THE FIVE DIAMOND BRAND

Center Point
Large Print

Also by Nelson Nye and available from Center Point Large Print:

The Texas Gun
Deadly Companions
Bancroft's Banco
The Wolf That Rode
The Leather Slapper

THE FIVE DIAMOND BRAND

NELSON NYE

CENTER POINT LARGE PRINT
THORNDIKE, MAINE

This Center Point Large Print edition
is published in the year 2025 by arrangement with
Golden West Inc.

Copyright © 1941 by Nelson Nye.

All rights reserved.

This book is a work of fiction. All names, characters,
places, and events are either products of the author's
imagination or used fictitiously.

The text of this Large Print edition is unabridged.
In other aspects, this book may vary
from the original edition.
Printed in the United States of America
on permanent paper sourced using
environmentally responsible foresting methods.
Set in 16-point Times New Roman type.

ISBN: 979-8-89164-638-4

The Library of Congress has cataloged this record
under Library of Congress Control Number: 2025936624

FOR
My Uncles
ROY AND CARO P. LATHAM

THE FIVE DIAMOND BRAND

Chapter One
A MAN GOES BACK

Off yonder, smoothed and flattened by the haze of distance, lay all the color and the glory of the Superstitions; land of faded trails, rusted picks and shovels; of gaping-windowed, roofless, empty, weather-bitten shacks; land of dust and memories. There was nostalgia in the view for the man on this big horse; all his life Ben Taylor had lived with tales of the roaring yesterdays when forty thousand campfires had turned the night skies red as paint, when twice that many sweating hombres had toiled and schemed and cursed and brawled for the precious metal locked in these mountain fastnesses, when ten-night towns had shrieked and shouted and life had been the cheapest thing in two hundred miles of wasteland.

Tradition of that kind rooted deep. The life was gone like the stage lines, like the Indians and the buffalo they hunted. But the memory of it lingered, coloring yet this land's activities. Cowhands still rode; they still swapped tales of bandits, talked of cattle, tough broncs, women. Crusty, wrinkled damned old fools prowled now as then the obscure, stone-choked canyons for the priceless pot they still believed lay at the rainbow's end. Only the spirit was different; only the manner changed.

Humans, Ben reflected, were likely much the same as Abraham had found them back in Biblical times. The same lusts governed them, the same intrigues and symbols. The same greeds still urged to thievery, the same desires to violence. The open-handed days were done, but the world had not changed much.

Mile-long shadows were bending across the range, and the late afternoon breeze was tugging the hair beneath his pushed-back hat and sending its remembered murmur curling through the gray-brown grasses, when Ben Taylor turned in the saddle, facing front once more.

His glance, gone quietly thoughtful, roved ahead with a lazy, all-seeing vigilance—a care that had thus far continued to keep him in the stirrups. It was a desperate game he played, a long-odds game in a quick-tempered country. The region may have gone to seed, the old blood thinned and cooled; but it was the self-same land, the self-same blood that had staged the hectic past.

Weltering in its heat down there, crouched in the farthest reaching of the mountains' tumbled slopes, so obstructed by the tangled crags the morning's sun must pass it over even as man's traffic seemed to have done for lo these many years, lay all that remained of the outlaws' rendezvous—Thief River. A drink-less trickle, gone stagnant and gone shallow. Three gray buildings squatted at the water's edge where the trail swung down from the hills through a littered, cracked dry wash. Just those, and the aged bones of a pole corral. All else was gone, howled away by the desert winds.

Those buildings were a landmark, monument to a departed era, showing little change in all the years he'd known them. Oh, a bit more gray, perhaps; a little more gaunt, more ramshackle. Essentially, though, they were not much different than when he, as a boy, had known each post and knothole. This land's ways had caught them, imbuing them with something of the spirit of its people, rugged, rancorous, and unmoved.

That great old barn of a place, the trading post, for instance. Warped and twisted by the years, but not a jot more than his memory of it. Wind and weather seemed impotent to affect it, as though long since they'd done their worst and now, scowling, muttering, reluctantly passed it by. Thief River's largest structure, it more than ever reminded him of some old tobacco warehouse, along the front of which some gay dog of a bolder day had built a railed veranda. He could almost hear its floorboards creaking now . . . the way they'd creaked the night Ace Yettem's crowd had lynched that horse-faced revenuer. An ugly, shameless, rowdy veranda leaning tipsily against the store and, with its crazy sagging roof, giving the appearance of a surly, leering cowhand made belligerent by an overload of booze. A morgue to buried hopes, that place; its groceries heir to dry rot, its liquor called so only by a courtesy as formidable as the courtesy governing its denizens' actions.

There was this combination bar and general store, a blacksmith shop, and the dilapidated remnants of what once had been a hostelry, which even yet played occasional host to a visiting brand inspector, or a man newly on the dodge. The rest was gone; yet the folk in this high country called these relics "town"—did their shopping, did their lounging here.

There were loungers on the store porch now, watching him, inscrutable.

He raised an arm in greeting, expecting no answer, getting none. They were not demonstrative people. Neither they nor the shadowy drifters pausing for a night or two had any use for convention. They had their own queer code and those who did not like it could do the other thing.

Taylor knew this yet always gave them that quiet politeness. It was a part of *his* system; and afterwards he surveyed them briefly with his dark, disconcerting stare. His mouth ends twisted with a kind of humor as he urged the big roan forward by gentle pressure of his knees.

He was tall, this young Ben Taylor; a tall man

and a brown one though he wore the gambler's rig. His hands were lean and tapered, long-fingered and powerfully swift. He was a man to remember, with his stubborn jaw and sandy hair. The whip of the wind was in his eyes and desert glare had baked his face and put an added whiteness on the teeth that showed through his tight, streaked smile. His seat in the saddle advertised its condition and told you much of the man himself—like the handle of his gun.

An easy bending of the knee stopped his horse before the store. He lounged, digging out the makings, for though he was a native of this country he had his manners well in hand. It was not considered courtesy to light down before being asked.

He got no invitation. The store-front loungers were watching him with a patent care, some aroused instinct somberly staining the taciturn slanting of their cheeks. And Monk Ide's hand was casually draped within two inches of his hip.

Taylor's glance assimilated these things, easily, completely; his mind digesting them at once. Long acquaintance with this section gave him key to their meaning, but he could not guess the motivation back of it.

Nor did he try to.

He swung a look at Jesse Hawes. The corral-keeper's short, broad shape hung against the store's gray wall with a sledge-like kind of solidness and returned a straight gray stare that had no friendship in it.

This was not like Hawes. There'd been a time—
"Nice trip?"

Ace Yettem's heavy-booted voice, smashing reflection instantly.

Taylor's turn was controlled, deliberate. He gave the man a cool and searching scrutiny. "Throwin' that music at me, Ace?"

They had never cared for each other much, these two. Yettem's brash manners, his scorn for the accepted way of things, his paraded shooting talent, heavy-handed sneers and patronage went against Ben Taylor's grain. On his part, the older man resented Taylor's youth, his growing stature and his refusal to take Yettem seriously; perhaps, even, the thing went deeper than that. Tall and gaunt, Ace Yettem was a rawboned product of the feuding Kentucky hills who'd come storming into this country a long while back and made himself at home. His heavy shock of hair took color from the carrot; the bony, sunburned face was freckled and, just now, was being turned slowly right and left in an elaborate show of searching. He said abruptly: "I don't see nobody else yere that's been p'rambulatin' 'round."

A smile touched Taylor's lips remotely. "Trip was all right, I guess. Had a pretty good run—"

"You still puttin' out to be a gamblin' man?"

The derisive curl of his lips had some foundation. Ben Taylor did make money gambling, but few would ever believe it who did not take a good look into his eyes. His rig called the guise a fiction. The frock coat was a shade too tight across his broad high shoulders; his string tie gave his neck the look of wishing it were without it, and his grace was more that of a man accustomed to a saddle than a stool or low-backed chair. Only his hands were right—his hands and the cool inscrutability of his eyes. And even the hands were marred by scars and rope-burns. And the face was not right at all. It was too bronzed, for one thing. And the nose was hooked; in the past he'd had it broken and had not taken care with its patching. It was a fighter's high, flat face—of a kind to be found in cow-country, but seldom back of a faro bank, a monte table or wheel.

Taylor knew these things, had vainly tried to correct them. He wore a lot of turquoise to give him a foppish look, but all that trick had done for him was get him called "Turquoise" Taylor. He had to ride, and riding left its telltale marks; he'd gotten into tight corners and those had put their brand upon him also. He said to Yettem pointedly: "It's one way to make a living; an' you'd be surprised at the amount of folks, Ace, still takin' me for a sucker."

Yettem let that pass. "How long you figgerin' to be around *this* time?"

Taylor's glance went over him by inches. But

he said quietly enough: "Hard tellin'. Depends how long my cash holds out—"

"Or your gall," said Yettem plainly.

Taylor looked at him while a stillness gathered—a quiet through which these watching men's antagonism rolled against Ben like a wave, sharpening his perceptions, cocking his long lean muscles and hinting plainly in his absence someone's talk had turned these men against him. An edge of his glance brushed Hawes again, but the corral-keeper's face was an image hacked out of wood. If there was any friendship in him, he was keeping the fact to himself.

Taylor's look swung back to Yettem. Yettem said: "You heard about Abe Peyrolles?"

"What about him?"

"Sheriff come in last month with a posse an' lugged him off fer a hangin'."

"Who'd Abe hang?"

"He didn't." Yettem said it meaningfully, darkly, the menace in his stare riding high and bright. "It was Abe got hung—for rustlin'."

Taylor considered him reticently. And then at last he said, "I guess Abe had it coming. We all know Abe's been—"

"Who says so?"

That was Ide's sharp voice; Ide's hand laying white on a gun butt.

"There's been plenty of talk," Taylor said, very soft. "Mebbe Mace—"

"Fargo didn't have no hand in it!"

"An' it ain't only Abe," Yettem murmured. "Been a lot of guys ridin' fer falls. Tim Birchman, Galloway—Bucks Younger. There's a polecat smell around this country."

Taylor smiled. "Shouldn't wonder. Country wasn't named Thief River for nothing, don't seem likely. Where there's smoke there's bound to be some fire—"

"Jest what I was tellin' Snub Wolters," Yettem nodded, his stare gone very bright. "Hard luck's a-campin' some too close." A grate got into his voice and he asked again: "How long you figgerin' to be around yere?"

"Your interest in my comings and goings seems a mite un-neighborly, Ace."

"I don't give a damn about your comings—it's your *goin's* we're interested in." He shook free of his slouch against the wall; leaned forward. An urge to violence touched fire to his stare. "It's your *goin's* we're interested in!" he repeated harshly.

"Is that," Ben asked Yettem softly, "supposed to be important?"

"I reckon Birchman, Galloway, an' Younger found it so—I know goddamn well Peyrolles did." Yettem came three swift steps forward, crouched, bent hands splayed beside his pistols. "Every time you ride out of this country somebody gets their comeuppance!"

Chapter Two
MACE FARGO

There was no doubt in Taylor's mind that Yettem's words had been strung as a challenge; had there been such doubt a glance put on those others would have settled it. But a man experienced as Ben had no need to go beyond Ace Yettem's voice, beyond his words or tautened posture. It was all there; neat, compact—unavoidable as Death. Yet Taylor's hand did not reach hipward; nor did he, scowling, fling his body from the saddle to smash that look from Yettem's face. He stayed where he was and licked his cigarette, one sturdy knee hooked lazily around the horn.

He stayed where he was and smiled; smiled provocatively at the man's histrionics. Briefly amused, he said: "Remarkable what them mail-order courses can do now, ain't it? 'F I didn't know you so well, I'd swear you was tryin' to hustle these boys into guttin' my hog or somethin'." He shook his head, regret faintly riding through the glance with which he eyed them. "I allowed you had more savvy. Don't hardly seem like a man your age an' style would trim his caliber that way to hide behind the holsters of his friends." He said then, earnestly, "If it's that Horse Mesa deal that's riled you, come out like a man and say so—but don't waste your time riggin' up such tripe as that; these boys got too much sense to fall for it."

That talk caught Yettem off balance; sent him a half-step backward, cheeks corrugated, flushed with an angry confusion. He had never been to Horse Mesa in his life—and far as he knew, neither had Ben Taylor. But these others couldn't know that.

He was still trying to dope it out, still trying to get at the meaning back of that crack about holsters, when Taylor passed him, going into the store.

When he came out, three-four minutes later, he had a tow-sack full of groceries under his arm which he carried to his horse and lashed behind the saddle.

But in that space Yettem figured things out, saw how adroitly Taylor had turned the tables, lifting himself into safety and leaving Yettem snagged out on a limb. He had the wit to realize how that maneuver had made him ridiculous. He had a need for the good opinion of these fellows on the porch; and raging, furious, he snarled thickly: "Just a minute, Taylor!"

Taylor wheeled with a speed that shrank the loungers against the wall. Monk Ide, who'd been sitting on the steps, rolled over twice and came up whitely back of a post. Taylor said, "Very well,

Ace. If you want it that way, haul your iron."

In the frozen silence Yettem, caught again off guard, stood tangled in his own emotions, stood bug-eyed with his jaw gone slack. He'd meant to force the issue, had meant to show Taylor up for a bluffer. But Taylor, damn him, had started his tricks again. The swiftness of Taylor's challenge had caught Ace Yettem with spread hands spraddled by his holsters; shocked still and frantic—without the bounce to draw.

"Well," Ben said. "What are you waiting on?"

Had the fellow smiled at him that way ten minutes back, Yettem would have killed him—would certainly have tried. Now he stood there rigid. So recently as thirty seconds ago the lust to murder had been in him. The lust was still there, but tempered now by a strange, cold doubt; by the wonder if he'd be *able* to drop Ben Taylor. He'd been confident, eager to get it over. Now that confidence was whelmed by a wonder that fast was curdling into frightened certainty. Taylor intended to kill him! In Taylor's cold, pale glance, he read his invitation and his doom.

Yettem dared not put his hand to gun. And he could see that Taylor knew it; and that these watching others knew it, also. It was the bitterest knowledge in Yettem's life. He'd been so sure of his ability—so certain he had Taylor where he wanted him. This was the thought that scourged his mind: He'd called for a showdown and couldn't stomach it. These men would think him a coward; he'd never live this down. In front of all Thief River, he was being made a fool of. But he couldn't draw. To save himself he dared not.

He cursed the mockery of Taylor's stare; the contempt and scorn he read there. But he made no move. He could not forget how six months back, Lick Haines, one of his men—and a gent quick on the trigger—had almost in this identical spot tried to build Taylor into a planting. Outmaneuvered in the battle of wits, Lick had tried to bull things through in powdersmoke. He'd been planted for his trouble, and knowledge of this now was keeping Yettem's hands away from leather.

He wished the hell he'd recalled this sooner.

He altered his weight with a straining care. The held-back breath was choking him.

He became aware of sudden change—of a sudden shifting of attention. Whipping an edged glance around to the side, he observed a man coming down the wash on a lathered horse. Under kinder circumstances, Yettem would have furiously resented the fact that anyone could draw these loungers' interest from himself. But at the moment, his relief was almost audible. A quick peek slanchways disclosed the comforting fact that Taylor had forgotten him; like the others, Taylor was giving all his attention to the man on the walking horse.

It was Yettem's chance. Very quietly he slipped inside the store.

The newcomer stopped his sweat-streaked pony beside the hitch rack. A little tension, left over from Yettem's fiasco, clawed its way along the porch, grinding all expression off the watchers' faces, turning their eyes, gone prudently wooden, from this horseman to Taylor and back again.

The new arrival took in Taylor's presence. He said briefly: "How are you, Ben?" and without waiting for any answer, laid his smoldering, bitter glance upon the loungers. "Boys," he growled, "we got to organize—we can't put the thing off any longer. There's rustlers workin' this country again. They hit your herd yet, Meeker?"

Ham Meeker shook his head. He ran the Whip outfit over on the footslopes of Music Mountain and didn't dabble much in local politics. "Ain't seen no sign, Mace. 'Course, I ain't had no reg'lar roundup yet—"

Mace Fargo's shoulders moved with characteristic impatience. He was young, as young as Taylor and, the way he sat his saddle, looked to be well over six feet in his fancy, polished range boots. Muscles swelled the shirt about his neck and chest and arms; and his face was round with bold and lively features that gave it a rugged vitality, that gave it a certain handsomeness that, though flushed just now with anger, was arrogant and very sure. A yellow-haired man,

Mace Fargo. His lips showed the temper of him.

He said, interrupting Meeker, "Ever since I can remember—far back as 1900, there's been a lot of bellyachin' 'round the state about this county packin' guns. You'd think we was plannin' a filibuster on the rest of Arizona t' hear 'em talk. But we got a damn big county here, all cut t' hell-an'-gone with mountains, canyons, badlands; we pass what laws we like, an' I say it's goddamn lucky we *ain't* passed no anti-gun law like they have most places. They been tellin' over at Phoenix we're just a bunch of money-grubbin' Yankees that go larrupin' 'round like horseback arsenals just to rope in tourist trade. By God, I'd like a handful of them pot-gutted politicians over here a few days! You fellas realize, by God, I've lost upwards of a hundred an' fifty steers in the last half week?"

Out of the startled silence Steve Fontana drawled, "Killed or stole?"

"Stolen!"

"How they gettin' 'em?" Holders Hockaday wondered.

"I don't know—but I've had Kreel takin' tally an' his count shows a hundred an' forty-seven short of what—"

"I guess Five Diamonds can stand it. Always been more or less stealin' 'round this country," Fontana pointed out. "Place wouldn't seem like home—"

Fargo raked an intolerant glance across Fontana's freckles. "A man can stand the two-bit stuff if he's got to; but there ain't no outfit in this country can stand losin' a hundred an' fifty beeves at a crack! Trouble with you, Fontana, is you ain't a cattle-raiser. You ain't got no ambition an' never will have—be content to go on year in an' year out workin' for some other fellow. No skin off'n your nose if . . ." He quit talking abruptly, his dark glance resting on Ben Taylor. "You got a spread over west of here—how *you* makin' out?"

"Can't complain," Ben said. "I lose a little now an' then." He regarded the other thoughtfully. "What do you have in mind, Mace?"

"I propose to clean the damn thieves out of this country!"

"Take considerable doing," Holders Hockaday remarked; and Taylor murmured: "How you goin' to tell the big thieves from the little ones?"

Fargo, big, willful, intolerant of any views but his own, scowled at Taylor irritably. "A thief's a thief whether he takes one cow or forty." His solid chin reached forward. "By God, I'll clean 'em out like rats!"

"Kinda hard on hombres that ain't workin' for Five Diamonds," Fontana said with rare reflection. "Reckon a fella in my class'll jest nacherly be shoved on over with the little fellas an' the thieves."

Ham Meeker said: "Don't you want no neighbors, Mace?"

"If a man's got to have thieves for neighbors, he's better off without any." A bright, locked stubbornness showed in Fargo's stare. "All you boys that are hirin' hands be out at my place tonight for supper. We'll get this thing thrashed out an' find where the hell we're at here." He rubbed his willful glance on Taylor. "You better be there, too."

Taylor took a last drag from his cigarette; snapped it into the road.

" 'Fraid not, Mace. I've other fish to fry."

"Meanin' you just won't come, eh?" The big man's stare showed a hot distrust.

"If you want to put it that way—yes."

"Now look," Ham Meeker said; "we ought to stick together—"

"If that's the way you see things, Ham, you follow your convictions. Mob psychology never appealed to me."

Fargo's face showed flushed and angry. "There'll be no swingin' over later—"

Taylor's laugh cut through his words. "I guess Fontana called the turn. There'll be no neutrals, either."

Fargo's eyes slashed Taylor roughly. "What the hell you mean by that?"

"A sentiment like yours turned loose can end up just one way. If you force folks into takin' sides, you'll turn these mountains into a bloody shambles—"

"Then let 'em *be* a shambles! If you'd lost—"

"If I lost a hundred an' fifty steers I'd certainly keep my eyes skinned out to find the guy—"

"Guy!" Fargo shouted. "Are you tryin' to tell me *one lone guy* got off with that many critters?"

"Wouldn't surprise me any," Ben said quietly.

"Why, God damn it! No rustler workin' solo—"

"Hold up a minute. You got any proof more than one fella was mixed up in it? Cut sign on 'em? *See* '*em?*"

Mace Fargo said impatiently: "You know I got too big a range—"

"There you are; you admit the fact yourself. You got 'too big a range.' Give your head a chance, Mace. Look at this thing reasonably. You don't suppose rustlers go larrupin' 'round in bunches like they used to, do you? Waitin' for a dark night, mebbe, or a storm to do their liftin'? This is nineteen-forty, man! There's more beef bein' taken in broad daylight than was *ever* shoved off in the old days by a bunch of shoutin' tarp-wavers."

Hockaday, owner of the 3 Rings iron, had been gnawing reflectively on a manicured left index finger. His eyes, that had been watching Taylor every moment of that talk, showed an odd, faint-shining humor. "Just a minute, Mace," he said. And to Taylor: "Let me get this straight, Ben.

You allowin' not more'n two-three fellows are responsible for them Five Diamonds steers takin' wing?"

Without taking his glance away from Fargo, Taylor said: "I'd say off-hand there was two. Doubt if all those critters were run off at once; I'm sure they were never all moved from one locality. Something wrong with the tally somewhere; if Mace has lost that many steers—"

"Are you callin' me a liar?"

"Certainly not." Ben met his furious stare with a cool directness. "But with the methods they're usin' now, no rustler—"

"What methods?" Hockaday interrupted.

"Rustlers," Ben said grimly, "have reupholstered their business—put it on a streamlined cash-an'-carry basis that'll earn a man who doesn't overwork himself ten thousand bucks a year." He paused to let that thought sink in, ignoring the scowls and incredulous looks that stamped his listeners' faces. "Rustlers are smarter than they used to be. They don't waste time and energy switchin' brands any more. They take stuff just as they find it and either butcher it on the spot or load it into covered moving vans and sashay on their way."

"Trucks, eh?" Ham Meeker said after a moment. "How they get 'em in there?"

"Hell, they carry salt to put on their tails," Mace sneered. "Of all the crazy—"

27

"It's not so crazy as you might think," Ben said, ignoring his sarcasm. "One or two fellas will get hold of a truck, load in a saddled horse apiece and go hunt them up a nice secluded piece of range—and by secluded, I don't necessarily mean some brushy place back in the hills; mostly these motorized rustlers grab up stuff along the highways. There are plenty of spots where there's sixty to a hundred miles between towns. Inside forty minutes a couple of skilled hands can rope and load in ten-twelve steers. Don't take 'em more than a couple seconds to close the drop door, an' then *off they go,* fifty-sixty miles an hour. Long before you've missed your steers—if you ever do—those boys have delivered them to a packing plant, gotten their money and vanished."

No one said anything for a bit. Mace Fargo was scowling darkly, considering this and not liking it, when Hockaday said abruptly: "How they get them brands by?"

"Same way," Ben said, "they get by sheriffs and Association men should such a person happen to stop them—by using forged papers. Forged bills-of-sale and stolen license plates are as much a part of these new bandits' equipment as a truck or lass-rope is. Most cases, naturally, the buyer knows these steers are lifted property and cuts his price according. But what's six or eight bucks less to a man who only had to rope and ride them?"

"Suppose," said Hockaday thoughtfully, "I caught a couple of these rubber-tired rustlers loadin' off my range? Be a corpse-an'-cartridge occasion like in the old days, wouldn't it?"

"I doubt it. Your rustlers would be a heap more apt to shove their broncs inside the truck, slam up the door an' bolt. No profit to them in fighting when they can cut their stick an' run. Quick's they quit your sight, they'd dump your cattle and split the breeze for calmer parts. If you went to the trouble of callin' the nearest authorities—say askin' a sheriff to stop them, he'd get laughed at for his trouble. They'd have an empty van with nothing to show they'd even *thought* of swiping your critters. If you were crazy enough to prosecute, you wouldn't get to first base."

"Suppose he didn't catch 'em then, but some smart tin-badge happens to get suspicious an' asks to look inside their van," said Meeker. "Mebbe he puts on to be a fruit or corn inspector, or mebbe a sheriff actin' for 'em. Got those waddies dead to rights then, ain't he?"

"Not unless he's grabbed a green hand. Most of the guys that are workin' this racket are plenty shrewd and able. They'll tell him they bought the stuff from you on behalf of the Drag 7, mebbe, over at the other side of the Pecos. The sheriff will fetch out his brand book and discover that, sure enough, there *is* a Drag 7 over there. He'll ask for their bill-of-sale then and they'll pass it over, everything filled in, including your name as owner. The name of the Drag 7 owner in the sheriff's book will tally with the name as buyer on their paper. The sheriff can't know—or prove, should he suspect it—that that ain't your signature at the bottom; he can't hold that truck while he goes into correspondence. The Drag 7 will never see those steers, but your law officer has nothing at hand to prove it."

"All that may be so," growled Fargo, "but I'm short my count a hundred an' forty-seven steers. I guess I know how many cattle I got! An' by God, that ain't the count I had when we finished branding! Those steers were taken in the last four days—"

"If they were, then there's more than one truck working on your stuff; and if there is, that means this thing is organized—that several outfits have got together and—"

A tide of color surged across Mace Fargo's cheeks. It jumped his pugnacious jaw belligerently forward and clenched his fists and smashed one of them thumping into the opened palm of the other. "You're goddamn right they have! That's what I said first off before you started slingin' that fancy gab. An'—"

"That," said Taylor coldly, "ain't no excuse for startin' a general range war in these mountains."

"It ain't, eh?" Fargo's eyes slashed Taylor bitterly. "Lemme tell you somethin', bucko. There's just two sides to this business: them that's doin' the stealin' an' them that's bein' stole from." There had never been much love lost between this man and Taylor; their antagonism had been born in them, inherited from the past. Taylor's father had been a marshal in Thief River and in the course of duty had shot a couple of Fargo's uncles—had put Fargo's father back of bars. And Fargo hadn't forgotten. Nor had things been helped when Fargo, in their school days, had decided sport meant bullying a nester kid and Ben had soundly thrashed him for it. Nor had Taylor's acquirement of a choice bit of rangeland over Fargo's bid improved their relations any. And then . . . there was a girl.

The memory of these things rolled across Mace Fargo's cheeks and he said gratingly: "I want to know right now, Ben, where you're standin'. You sidin' these cow-thievin' sons or us?"

Chapter Three

"WHEN YOU LEAVE THIS TOWN—"

"Us?" Ben Taylor said.

Fargo's face was flushed and irritated. "The honest ranchers of this country. The men who've worked for what they've got—" He broke off with a scowl at Taylor's smile, then went on doggedly: "Men like me an' Hockaday an' Meeker."

"Aren't you including Yettem?"

Fargo pulled up his chin and stared. His face got ruddier than usual and a furious, balked anger squeezed his eyelids down to slits through which the eyes themselves gleamed hotly with a pale and wicked flame. He sat his saddle that way, very still—all the bitter, turbulent feeling of him savaging his cheeks; then wheeled his horse without a word and roweled it through the river, sending the water splashing and leaving a quiet back of him that held no relaxation.

Meeker, irritated, said at last: "Where was the sense, Ben, rakin' him up like that? We know you're with us. Why—"

"Am I?" Taylor said. "Get this straight, you fellows. I'm not with anyone—certainly not with any *bunch*. I don't like a cow thief any more than the rest of you, but before I'll take any action against a man I'm going to have to see him rustling with my own eyes—I'm not taking another guy's word for it."

Monk Ide said, "You always was partial to pickin' a diff'rent side from Mace—"

"Where he stands ain't got a thing to do with the way I trail my bets. I'll say this, though: I'm not breakin' out in any lather to build him into a cattle king—"

"You think he's got ideas that way?"

"What I think, Ide, needn't concern you. This country's big enough for all of us; it's not big enough for a dictator."

Ide smiled queerly in that dark, thin way he had. But if he'd found humor in Taylor's words he made no offer to share it. Getting up he whacked the dust from his Levi's and walked over to his horse. A few moments later he rode off into the south. Ham Meeker said: "Then you don't think over a couple gents is workin' on these cattle?"

"That's my opinion," Taylor answered. "But if I'm wrong, mass action such as Fargo wants is not the way to—"

"What *is* the way?" asked Hockaday.

"I don't know. Seems like getting in touch with the Association—"

"I've appealed to them before," growled Hockaday with rancor. "There's no use goin' to them.

The crooks around this country savvy every move the Association's got in mind before they ever get it started. You can't lick this racket that way."

"Well, you'll never lick it with Fargo's plan. My advice would be to—"

"You always was a bunch-quitter," Hockaday said.

Ben caught him up like a shot. "I never belonged to any bunch to start with. I don't need any gang at my back to take care of *my* interests, Hockaday. If a man ain't big enough to stand on his own feet by the time he's twenty-one, he's got no business out here."

"Is it standin' on *your* feet," Hawes asked softly, "that takes you out of sight so frequent?"

Yettem's poison. Taylor knew this and could find no way to deal with it. There were things that he might do but they could not wipe out or even adequately counteract the effect of Yettem's tongue. God only knew what the fellow had been hinting while Ben had been away.

A faint regret turned the lines of his face briefly somber, seeing that hard light in Hawes' gray stare. It spelled an end of much that was pleasant; of long nights passed in cards and chess and talk of range conditions, of traded reminiscences made warm, made intimate by grace of Bella's company. But that end was here. Hawes was erecting a monument to it now.

"Just what," he asked, "are you hinting, Jesse?"

"I'm hintin' you know a sight too much about the way these rustlers work. An' my name to you hereafter," said Bella's father, without compromise, "is Hawes."

Very still, Taylor's glance scoured the corral-keeper's cheeks. And at last, reluctantly, narrowed, it raked the faces of those watching others. They were all of a piece, save only that that dark, faint-shining humor still was coloring Hockaday's stare.

Looking at Hawes again he nodded.

White-mustached, handsome and a little elegant in tan trousers, blue coat and tall white Stet-hat among these overalled others, Hockaday said: "Better run a tally on your calf crop, Taylor."

"Thanks—I will," Ben told him grimly, and put a hand up to the horn.

He was lifting his foot to stirrup when Fontana's soft drawl crossed the silence. "Hold up. I've got to go your way, Ben. Just a second; I'll ride with you."

"Better not. You might get—"

"I'll take my chance on that," Fontana grinned, and gave those others a skeptical, slanchways eying. "Country's come to a hell of a pass if a man can't pick his saddlemates. Anyhow, I reckon I'm numbered with the goats already. Ridin' with you won't hurt me."

He walked to his horse and Taylor swung up in the saddle.

"When you leave this town," said Hawes, very grim and earnest, "don't come back."

Chapter Four
A FORCED INVITATION

It was around 3 o'clock in the afternoon, with a sullen banner of dust boiling out of the valley that lay like a shining white platter between Thief River and the eight-mile-distant Goldfield Mountains, when Bella Hawes, shrugging ruefully, left the backyard smashing of the brutal sun to the sand and wasps that appeared to thrive on it and wheeled discouragedly into the doubtful improvement of the old hotel which, years ago, the last proprietor had deeded her father in exchange for two fast broncs. There was no use trying to cultivate roses in Arizona—certainly not in Thief River, at any rate!

She was a slender girl, a bit above the average in height, with a body utterly synchronized and with a skin the hottest day left pale. Her lips were full and red and curving across a face made warm and personal by the frank curiosity bequeathed her by a mother she had never known. Her poise, her calm serenity, came from nineteen years of being her father's daughter; of caring for him, living with him, of sharing his work and problems. She had his eyes and something of his reticence—his uncanny skill with horses; but never the godlike attribute of judgment that had so narrowed his outlook. Their hard and lonely life bred reticence—bred narrowness of outlook, too, and might have warped her own—it and the old man's rigid code—had she not possessed the redeeming gift of laughter. She was like Fontana that way: she could find a humor in life's ironies.

Her handiwork had made a living room of the hotel's shabby lobby and, passing into it now, she paused before the glass above the mantel to run deft fingers through the disarray of jet-black curls before sitting down to resumption of Louis Bromfield's "Night in Bombay." It was a good book and she had been enjoying it; but now the vicissitudes of its characters failed to rouse concern in her, their problems could not hold her, for there were suddenly in Thief River problems more personally touching her, more deeply affecting her with their threat of change, of anguish.

She was a thinking girl and there was, of late, a great deal in this country to be thought about. The rising insolence of that gun-quick outlander, Yettem. The strange, dark moods that were lately governing Mace Fargo, that were becoming so much a part of him and that were driving him more cruelly even than his lust for power and overweening ego to some dark, fantastic end. Nor were these all. There was her father's increasing grimness, increasing taciturnity; and the riddle of

Ben Taylor's mysterious trips. It was this last that bothered her most.

Where did he go when he rode off into the mountains? What desire or need or danger was taking him more frequently away from his ranch and dropping him from sight among the trackless wastes of the badlands? What agency was responsible for the new and strange aloofness that was stripping Ben Taylor of past friendships? For the sharpened edge so recently noticeable in his keen-eyed stare? For the rift in this man's relations with her father?

Where did he go, and for what purpose?

It all came back to that. Men were speculating and queer rumors were adrift. Their muttered whisperings alarmed her, filled her with unwonted apprehensions. What was he up to? Monk Ide last month had tried to trail him—vainly; all sign had petered out southeast of Sawik Mountain.

Sawik Mountain! What had taken Ben over there? There were no ranches worthy of the name in that vicinity; a harsh, uncared-for country, roamed by only Indians. What hidden interest could have taken him so far off the beaten track? A mine? There was gold in Paradise Valley, in that desolation between McDowell Mountain and Thompson Peak.

She recalled uneasily a rumor started recently by Yettem. He'd been talking over whisky in the trading post with Kreel, Mace Fargo's foreman. It would not be difficult, he said, for a man who knew this country thoroughly to dispose of stolen cattle to the Indians at Salt River Reservation.

An ugly hint, compatible with the character of its sponsor. The Salt River Indian Reservation encompassed that bleak country into which—by Monk Ide's say-so—Ben Taylor's trail had vanished.

What did she know of Ide? Very little, was the conclusion reached of her pondering; very little save that the man was often seen in Yettem's company, and that he had a small place somewhere among the rocks of Rogers Canyon. What he did for a living, whether he ran cows or horses, she had no idea.

No more idea than she had of what Ace Yettem did. He had a ranch of some kind down in the Superstitions, and seemed to have a pretty big payroll if one could judge by the number of hard-faced men she'd seen in his company off and on. It was kind of queer, if you stopped to think of it, that more was not known about him; but his movements, like his business, seemed well wrapped in that fog-like murk of reticence that obscured the status of so many of this region's denizens—a sly, back-country flotsam, men of buried pasts and small connivings.

A casual look through the window disclosed the store veranda to be littered with the usual after-noontime loungers. Meeker, Ide and Holders Hockaday; and Steve Fontana whom everybody knew had no better use for the time he had than to sit like an addle-pated halfwit, abstractedly tallying the breeze-livened movement of the juniper-cast shadows that fluttered across the road. She'd seen him sit by the hour with that quaint smile on his mouth, listening with that far-off look in his eyes to the wind's song blown through long dead grasses. He was—to quote Mace Fargo—"a barnacle on the rump of progress," and it was Hockaday's opinion that "If it wasn't for havin' to eat, that bird would never lift a hand!" An odd man, Steve. A wistful one. Mostly, people liked him.

She wondered what he found to think about, always lolling 'round like that with his humorous eyes squinting off into space through the lazy patterns his forgotten cigarette created on the drowsy afternoon air.

Then, presently, she was watching Ace Yettem come riding in with another man; watching her father saunter across to join the benchwarmers on the porch. Talk got a bit more spirited; even Fontana appearing to rouse himself and listen. It looked like Yettem was doing most of it, and once in a while when one of the others would throw in some remark he would gesture violently. Then talk quit suddenly and all eyes swung abruptly to the east.

Bella looked that way; and a quicker interest fired her glance as she glimpsed the approaching horseman. No other man in all this country rode with such quiet grace. It was Ben Taylor coming back from one of his trips.

In that moment all the vague disquiet and unrest gathered during his absence dropped away from her. Then it caught her with a tightened clutch as she saw the still, grim watching of those men upon the porch; saw Taylor's raised arm drop unanswered. There was something secret, prohibiting, hostile in the attention of those men. The book slipped from her lap and she leaned forward, suddenly breathless.

Yettem spoke and she saw Monk Ide's hand fixed to back him. Ben said something she could not catch. A malicious grin quirked Yettem's lips. His shouted words were almost hissing in their malignance: "Every time you leave this country somebody gets their comeuppance!"

Bella's breath choked in her throat. A kind of paralysis rooted her to the window. She tried to close her eyes but could not. Fighting talk; in this quick-tempered land those words were a challenge to unbridled violence, and she looked in agony to see Ben Taylor's hand go leaping down to leather.

Startlingly, Taylor made no move of any kind. He sat where he was, eying Yettem with the tolerance a grown person accords the antics of a child; and, suddenly, a thin smile put expression on his face, changed the set of his cheeks to a derisive slanting. She heard his drawled words with a lifting admiration. How easily, how coolly and effectively he was putting Yettem in the wrong!

She took a deep breath and looked at Yettem. The gun-thrower had gone a half-step backward, his face disturbed, flushed and angry and confused. He was still that way when Taylor passed him, going into the store.

In a few moments she saw Taylor coming out again. He had a sack of purchases which he lashed behind his saddle.

She left the window hurriedly. If Taylor intended going to his ranch he'd soon be passing the hotel, and she wanted to have a word with him before he quit the town.

But there was no point in apprising the town of this. Bella's lithe, free-swinging stride took her through the hotel's side-entrance. Where she waited for Ben beside the shaggy yuccas, the store could not be seen; and the men's voices reached her only as a subdued murmur, unintelligible, low, monotonously purring as the droning of the flies.

She could not think what was keeping Ben. If he were going to his ranch he should be passing here. The minutes dragged; she had not guessed they could be so long. Had he gone off someplace else? But she hadn't heard his horse . . .

And then she did hear horse sound—the wicked, rushing pound of flying hoofs; heard them splash across the river, heard them swiftly dim in distance.

What had happened? Why had he gone rushing off that way? Why had he gone tearing south when his ranch lay due northwest? Why hadn't he crossed at the ford as he always crossed?

Puzzled, astonished and a little hurt, she was about to turn back into the hotel when she became aware the murmur of men's voices no longer broke the quiet. The cross-trails hamlet lay still as though the last warped soul had left it.

Why?

It were as though the shadow of death hovered over that group before the store. Born and raised in this grim country, she was not without acquaintance with that violence that had made its past—not without some knowledge of how swift an ill-chosen word might culminate in gunsmoke.

Her cheeks showed blanched and frightened; there was tumult in her breast. Had those larruping hoofs heralded some other man's departure? Someone other than Taylor? Had someone shot him and fled away while those others at the store watched wooden-faced?

She had heard no shot . . . But perhaps a knife had been the means! She was clutched by a fear the like of which she'd never known. Her knees were trembling, her hands and body shaking. But she could not help it; she could not think coherently.

Perhaps Ben was not yet dead. Perhaps he lay, dust-covered, bloody, writhing in his anguish—needing her. She must not fail him!

Though he'd never breathed a word, she knew he loved her; knew instinctively he did, just as she loved him and always had as far back as memory went. She recalled in that grim moment how, back in their school days he'd made faces at her, called her a tomboy—how he'd taken a perverse delight in snapping spitballs at her from behind his piled-up books.

She must go to him—must hurry. But first she must fortify herself, must steel herself against the avid eyes of those always watching, always present porch loungers. They must not guess—

She stopped, brought up and stiffened. Dust-muted sound of walking horses drifted to her from the street, came to her and left her rigid, breathless—afraid to go, afraid to linger. And then Ben's voice, low, admonishing, came to her, and Steve Fontana's, lazily indifferent, making humorous answer to something Ben had said.

Bella trembled in the cold, reacting clamp of sudden relief. She leaned, wholly weak, against the doorpost; struggling desperately to compose herself.

She could see them now; they were rounding the gray, initial-carved boarding of the hotel's corner, Ben looking a little grave and Steve Fontana still chuckling. They saw her then and Ben was nodding, and Steve dragged off his hat and with a muttered something turned his horse aside while Ben came on.

He stopped the roan beside her and sat there, getting out the makings and eying her with that remembered whimsicality, with that familiar lopsided twisting of his long hard lips. " 'Lo, tomboy," he said. "Good tree-climbin' weather—if a fella was the climbin' kind. Who chiseled the silver linin' off your Paw's best cloud?"

She looked up at him quickly to see if he were joking; but he wasn't. Behind that easy smiling there was something in his glance she could not read. Something grim and dark and probing. He said before she could question him: "What's the matter, Bella? You look—"

She said, "I thought—But never mind. Who left town in such a hurry?"

"Why, that was Mace. Mace Fargo, Bella. He come for a chunk of fire an' was scared he'd have to take it. Nothin' for you to go an' get upset about. Jesse ailin'?"

"He hasn't said anything. What makes you think so?"

Taylor shrugged, looking off beyond her, his dark glance probing the gloom of the hotel hallway while he struck a match to his cigarette. "These people," he said, "that's been tellin' the country the West is dead, have got a kind of surprise in store for 'em. Mace been confidin' in you lately?"

She shook her head. "Mace isn't confiding in folks these days. Kind of favors you that way. Did you have a good trip?"

His long cool look pulled color to her cheeks. "That what's tramped Jesse's bunions up? Expect it's been botherin' Mister Yettem, too. He seemed quite exercised about it. It's funny, Bella, how folks'll worry so over things that don't concern them—"

Bella, fighting temper, said quickly: "You needn't think, Ben Taylor, *I'm* trying to pry into any of your secrets! What you do an' where you go—"

"Sure—sure; I know. You ain't interested a bit. Trouble is, some of these other folks 'round here ain't got your balance. You know—" he gave her his quick-streaked grin, "you're a mighty fetchin' baggage, Bella—*mighty* fetchin'."

She flushed, half frowned; like so many times in the past not quite sure of how to take him. Perhaps it was carried-over reaction from her fright that made her say, a little spitefully: "If you want to spend all your time over 'round Sawik Mountain—" She stopped, a little flustered, a little sorry now that the words were out. The change that ran its shadow across his high, flat cheeks made her definitely uneasy. Nor did his easy words reassure her greatly.

"So that," he murmured, eying his cigarette with an unaccustomed care, "is what was back of Yettem's play." He looked up with his long lips faintly curving. "How your roses coming? Been doin' any better since you tried that fertilizer?"

She shook her head, checked what she'd been about to say, and said instead: "I guess this country's too hard for roses."

He nodded gravely. "It's a hard country, Bella—harder than most folks realize. There's a lot of stuff down under the surface, smolderin' like the hot coals left behind a prairie fire. A hard country; an' it'll be gettin' worse before it gets any better. Well, Steve's waitin'. Guess I better shove on."

She said quickly: "There'll be a dance at Tortilla schoolhouse Friday night . . ." She stopped, surprised, a little hurt by the quick sobering of his look.

He did not speak at once and she turned abruptly, staring off down the road, resentful of the suddenly heightened color that was giving her thoughts away. She wished she had not mentioned the dance. The need assumed a lesser stature than it had worn before she spoke. But he'd been away—wouldn't have known; and she had to go. Every girl in miles would be there. And she'd wanted Ben to take her. Three or four months ago she'd have mentioned it as she had just now and thought nothing of it. And Ben would have asked her right away. Why wasn't he asking her now?

The dragging seconds were slow as crawling caterpillars. Why didn't he speak? Why didn't he say something? Why didn't he ask her to go with him? What was wrong? What had caused this change in him? Was it related to those mysterious trips? Why should she feel embarrassed over mentioning that dance?

And then he said rather oddly, "Guess Mace'll be takin' you, won't he?"

"Mace?" She flushed a little and the nails of her fingers dug into her clenched palms. "No. Mace won't be taking me because I've already told him I was going with you."

There was a little silence then. She didn't look at him because she couldn't face him in that moment. Not for worlds would she let him see how much she cared. Perhaps he *had* known about that dance; perhaps he'd asked some other girl and that was why—

He said: "Shucks, that was mighty thoughtful of you, Bella. I'll sure be mighty proud to take you. Be callin' for you Friday night—"

She turned then, shoulders back, chin up, her eyes very bright and distant. "No—I guess you'd better not. I've changed my mind. I don't think I shall go—"

"Not go?" He looked at her, startled. "Why not? Why in thunder wouldn't you go? You can't stay home. Every girl in a hundred miles—" His eyes got sharp, got searching. "Of course you're going. Do you think—Why, I wouldn't miss a chance like this for a million. Be like old times—"

"Please, Ben. I'd rather not."

"Nonsense. Stuff an' nonsense. I'll be after you about eight-thirty," he said, and swinging the roan about, he went loping after Fontana. But his grin had been a little forced and his eyes had not grinned at all; all the time he talked, he'd seemed to be remembering something, and the aspects of that memory kept her standing there, kept her thoughtfully looking after him till the horse took him out of sight.

She turned then, her own smile warped and worthless, to meet the cold gray stare of her father. Jesse Hawes stood just inside the hall's screen door and the slanting of his cheeks was wicked.

Chapter Five
TORTILLA SCHOOLHOUSE

The schoolhouse at Tortilla was no place near the fallen timbers of the one-time gold camp; it was a gaunt and solitary building of peeled and sun-whitened pine abandoned to the mercy of the elements among the waist-high junipers of a shallow mountain meadow. Stars flashed palely from a sky that was sheerest turquoise in the bright shade of its blue, and the moon-illumined clouds seemed scarcely to elude the reaching fingers of the limestone crags, so close, so low they looked to Ben and Bella. The night was cold with a gusty wind rolling off the peaks and the sagebrush orchestra was sawing away like the devil, shelving bodies as they pushed their way through the hitched horses, cars and wagons toward a cluttered doorway that was noisy with the boisterous talk and laughter of the men grouped 'round a whisky keg. Taylor said: "We'd like to get inside, boys," and enough of them altered their postures to allow him grudging footroom; but only two men spoke to him and both looked first at Bella before displaying that brief civility. A hard, reluctant courtesy that left her thoughtful, showing clear as anything could the change in Taylor's status. Then she caught Ace Yettem's stare and shivered.

Still gripped by that chill, and with the sardonic mockery she had glimpsed in Yettem's regard chasing all the joy from the evening, she let Ben guide her through the entrance. The inside confusion rolled against them, heated, hilarious, strong with the stench of body sweat, horses and breath from the keg outside. The racket was gigantic, monstrous, importunate in its demand upon the emotions; and all across the room's broad center gyrating couples were whirling beneath the paper lanterns and red streamers to the frenzied exertions of the flushed-faced fiddlers and whooping banjoists. Thief River making holiday.

A pile of benches shoved to a far corner held a collection of squalling infants whose contributions to the uproar added nothing to its harmony. Every available woman was out there on the floor and half a dozen long-geared hombres, too full of hell to wait their chance, had paired off into yipping couples and, like stampeding cattle, had taken over one whole end of the building.

Older folks swapped gossip along the bench-flanked walls and the bulge of watchers about the door grew steadily larger and tougher.

Bella grimaced. "Some crowd."

Taylor nodded. "Everyone an' his uncle. Won't

even be standin' room time a few more of these roughnecks squeeze in."

Following his glance as they swung in and out between the other dancers Bella observed how the crowd about the door had grown. A hard-faced crew for the most part, men she had not seen before; fellows from brushy backlands, she guessed, come into ogle the merrymakers and get their share of the barrel. And yet they did not quite look like ordinary ranch hands. She could not say just what it was that set them apart from the others but, glancing up at Ben, she discovered something of that same quality in his face. He was watching them over her shoulder.

She wondered if he knew them, and memory of Yettem's stare came back to haunt her, to rouse again that vague disquiet that of late had become so much a part of her waking hours.

There'd been something secret in that look; something malevolent, maliciously mocking. She was still endeavoring to make up her mind what the outlander's glance portended when another pair of dancers collided with them roughly.

"Sorry," Ben murmured, and without looking around wheeled her expertly into another group that showed a space less cluttered. Ordinarily Bella would have enjoyed this frolic; Ben was a good dancer and she liked the color and gaiety, the chance to renew old friendships that these jamborees afforded. But tonight, she could not put her heart into it. There was an undercurrent of tension, of edged expectancy that could not be ignored. The gaiety was forced—was much too blatant, too determined. These other women felt it, too. It had its fangs in their laughter. They showed restless, nervously excited, almost belligerently happy. They were dancing on a powder keg and everybody knew it.

But one thing Bella felt thankful for. Whatever happened, things ought to swing clear of the killing stage, for guns, with the hats of the men and the ladies' shawls, had been checked by request in the cloakroom. If there were lethal weapons in this crowd, they were weapons brought in deliberately, and without the doorkeepers' knowledge.

The music stopped and everyone clapped and there was a great deal of wild, loud cheering. Ben and she were near the doorway when someone bumped them again. It was deliberate. She knew it on the instant. A bronzed six-footer had rammed against them. He hulked now, arms akimbo, squarely in their path, eyes mocking, a leer stretching heavy lips. "Want the whole show, do you? Whyn't you watch where you're goin'?"

"Sorry," Ben said quietly. "My fault entirely. I apologize."

Other dancers leaving the floor had paused, were eying them narrowly. With a nod, Ben made to guide her past the man, but the fellow put an arm out, barring their way. "Hold on," he growled belligerently. "Mebbe you're sorry an' mebbe you ain't. But that ain't puttin' no shine back on my boots. Who the hell d'you think you are 'round this place anyway?"

The fellow's boots were old and scuffed, criss-crossed with chaparral scratches—dusty; if ever they'd known the feel of polish it had not been since he donned them.

But Ben said: "My name's Taylor. Treat yourself to a new pair and send the bill to the Two Bars ranch."

"Yeah? You don't look like no cattleman to me—you look like a goddamn *tinhorn!*"

Ben's smile amazed the girl even more than his lack of anger. He said: "I've got myself to thank for that. There's a style about a good frock coat I've never been able to resist. If you'll step aside now, friend, the lady would like a little air."

Slack-jawed, the man stood staring as Ben Taylor led her past. But glancing across her shoulder as Ben was guiding her through the door, Bella saw the fight-hungry specimen making toward Ace Yettem and, suddenly, she understood.

On a bench at the rear of the schoolhouse a plump and matronly woman was serving punch to the ladies. There was quite a group about her and, by the time Ben had got their drinks, the fiddles, mouth-harps and banjos were whooping it up again.

"Lot of dudes up here tonight. Dude wranglers, too," Ben said, "judgin' by the angora pants. Corner's crowd, I guess; I see his station wagon over there. Well," he grinned, "shall we give it another whirl?"

Fontana was lounging by the door toe-deep in an aimless conversation being sponsored by a freckled puncher with lavender sleeve elastics. Steve grinned as they approached. "Two Bars still where you left her?"

"Still there," Ben said.

"How's the Hockaday angle?"

Ben said drily: "That new grass works wonders."

"Mebbe you got generous neighbors. How's the hoof-shakin', Bella? Got your best shoes tromped to ribbons yet?"

"Pretty near," she laughed; but there wasn't any laughter in her heart. She did not understand Fontana's talk nor Ben's enigmatic answer—she scarcely heard them. She was thinking grimly: "What will happen next?"

And, suddenly, she had her answer.

Ace Yettem stood before her. There was a brash grin stretched across his sunburned features; a wisp of carrot hair dangled rakishly before his eyes. "Evenin', Bella. I'll be takin' that dance you promised."

"You got the wrong night, Ace."

Taylor said it softly, but the place went still,

surcharged with violence. Talk sloughed off in a widening pool about them and the light across men's faces gave the thing a touch of melodrama; taut they were, expectant, avid. The laugh died on Fontana's lips and three near men backed hastily off and Taylor's face was bone and skin with no expression on it. "You've got the wrong night, Ace," he repeated. His tone was civil, but no one felt in any doubt about his meaning.

"Have I?" That jubilant impudence fanned suddenly brighter in Yettem's jeering eyes. He brushed the hair off his forehead and spat, and a new, hard grin rocked the lips back across his teeth. "And how would any truck-loadin' rustler come to know that, Mister Taylor?"

There! It was out now. Someplace Yettem had found the guts to bring his hints and whisperings into the open. This was what they amounted to. Just this—that Ben Taylor was on the make. That he was stealing his neighbors' cattle.

Something was plain enough to Taylor then. He took a long time to shape his answer, and when he did, it was to say quite quietly, "That's the way you figure to play this hand, Ace, is it?"

It puzzled Yettem, wrinkling up his face and threatening to confuse him as Taylor's other words had confused him before the store. Then change with a hidden knowledge ran a new look over his features, a look that was confident, belligerently triumphant.

He said: "You're damn well right it is! Guess you reckoned you was pretty slick when your cows started droppin' twins. Too bad you couldn't have been a mite slicker; we found that beef you shoved in the canyon. You had your gall—Five Diamonds, every bit of it, an' not a goddamn brand changed!"

The night was lurid with that hemming gleam of watching eyes, each staring face set strongly in its expectation of explosion.

Taylor said: "Do you think these folks'll swallow that?"

"They don't have to swallow nothing. The proof of it is right there on your spread—what's more, we got your own word for the way you worked it. Trucks, you said, an' by God, trucks it was! We found a set of tire marks that didn't get rubbed out. What you got to say to that?"

Ben's glance rolled over them, cold, banked dark with interest. He did not know the men packed solidly back of Yettem. Monk Ide was there, and Kreel, Mace Fargo's foreman; but the rest of them were strangers, bronzed, dark-cheeked and grim of eye.

He got the makings, rolled and lit a cigarette and drew the smoke deep into his lungs. He tried to see the end of this and saw instead the way the lamplight illumined Bella's face, bringing out the blue-black luster of her hair, accentuating the dead-white pallor of her cheeks, and clawing him with the womanliness, the desirability of her. It played tricks with him, dangerously unsettling the needful run of his thoughts.

He must answer Yettem. But could he tell these men he hadn't been in this country lately. They knew that he'd been gone—knew it all too well. The question, if he was to help himself, was *where;* and he could not tell them that—at least, he would not. This plot was better than those others; it showed a nicety of timing, a care for detail that could never have found its source in Yettem's head. Yettem's was the task of pinning deadwood; and he'd been well chosen for this work with his hot, blind hate and driving jealousy.

"What? Ain't you goin' to deny it?" Yettem taunted.

"Why should I?" Ben said quietly. "You've got the stage all set, the—"

"No, you don't!" snarled Yettem. "You ain't palmin' it off onto me!" In a frenzy lest Taylor's talk should get him from their trap again, he flung caution to the winds and whirled, fists clenched, arms raised and trembling, glaring out over the crowd with blazing eyes.

"Boys—you men out there! You fellows know me; we've fought an' sweated side by side to get ourselves a stake in this man's country. Our folks have fought an' bled an' died tryin' to pile us up a heritage. For what? For some thievin' scut of a rustler to steal away in the night? By God, I tell you this Ben Taylor's nothin' but a cattle thief—a low-down, stinkin' rustler! An' I say we know what to do with—"

"That's a lie!" cried Bella fiercely, but her words were lost in the growl of men around her.

"He's a goddamn rustler!" Yettem shouted. "Ask him where he goes to all the time! He won't answer that, but *I* will: He goes northwest past Sawik Mountain—up into that Indian country beyond Salt River; an' by God, I say that's where our cattle are goin'!"

Yettem knew these men, these Thief River ranchers; knew them with his own sure cunning and by his own experience—knew what forces he'd be loosing when he hurled those shouted words. They were long-suffering men who hated any kind of rustler with every ounce of red blood in them. It was a rabble-rousing, sure-fire call to caveman instinct. He knew from past performance how the ethics of accepted social conduct would fade like fog before the wind once the lusts and hatred of this crowd was stirred, and he bent all his energies into stirring them. He wanted a mob—a mob that would do his bidding.

"There," he snarled, and flung his hand straight into Taylor's face—"There's the man responsible for the cattle we been losin'! Right there he stands! An' I say, by God, us boys know what to do with him!"

The beast was waking. A growl was rumbling in its throat. Taylor had to act—and *quick,* if he would save his life. He knew as well as Yettem did the ease with which a mob was roused. These people would never stop to think; they would act by instinct. Under the lashing spur of Yettem's tongue their prejudice, their blind emotionalism would be driven to precipitate, vengeful action. Their fury would be turned on him, and nothing then—no least thing under God, could save him. Already there were cries of "Rope!" Remembrance of past wrongs was tugging them. Their lifting voice was like the growl of rushing waters.

With malevolent calculation Yettem cried: "Are we goin' to wait till he steals us blind?"

It was then that Taylor acted. Yettem saw his whip-lean body coming. He was trying to move when Taylor's lashing fist exploded between his eyes.

That rocking blow stopped Yettem squarely in his tracks; it hung him there like a butchered steer, eyes glazed and body sagging; it flung him sack-like, stumbling, full into the startled crowd. It hushed the growls like a mighty blanket.

Bella clutched at a ceiling post, as stunned and speechless as the rest. It did not seem like a single blow could have downed a man like Yettem. But he was down all right. His body made a grotesque heap in the sand before the door.

Somebody raised a lantern and the blood showed plain on his face.

Fontana drew a long, admiring breath. He looked at Yettem with a large, pleased smile and muttered softly: "Well!"

Then Yettem was clawing upright with the blood dripping down his chin. He swayed there, groggy, red-eyed, muttering. He was like an abandoned marionette, sort of hanging there with his bony head queerly canted, with his knees half folded—wobbly. His breathing made a painful sound. It seemed to shake him with its rasping, and the stuff from his broken nose laced his shirt with a livid pattern.

He dragged the chin up off his chest. His rolling, bloodshot gaze took sudden focus. Realization hung its flag out and a look, brutally berserk, chased the last semblance of humanity from his features. With a wholly animal cry, he whipped a knife from someplace and with the same motion flung himself at Taylor.

Taylor blocked the wicked reaching of that blade with lifted elbow. He went half around, his turning shape completely graceful, perfectly timed. A pile-driver right exploded flush with Yettem's jaw. He struck again—and still once more before Yettem's legs buckled under him. Ruthless, mauling blows that packed terrific punishment; blows that smashed the outlander to his knees, to his back, to a still and crumpled heap.

Breaking the stunned silence, a man's broad shoulders came plowing through the jam; came recklessly and savagely, uncaringly sending men right and left as furrowed earth is rolled by a plow. He stopped directly in front of Taylor, planting himself there solidly on legs set wide apart. Lamplight made a mean, dark glitter of his eyes.

"That's far enough," he gritted. He said with terrible finality: "Don't lay your hands on him again."

Taylor's eyes met Fargo's brightly. "Seems like, Mace, you're takin' a powerful interest in this fellow. Why?"

"Never mind why!" snarled Fargo bitterly. "I pick what friends I please!"

"That's your right. But Yettem's a damn tough monkey. Not the kind I'd expect to find in your string."

"Never mind! I ain't askin' you to pick my friends." Darker color roused Fargo's sultry cheeks. "Stay out of my business an' keep your goddamn jaw off me—you hear? I don't want to hear no more of them cracks about cattle kings."

"I expect the boot fit pretty well—"

"Never mind. You play your hand an' I'll play mine."

Taylor said: "Better have a look where that hand is taking you—"

"What's that?"

"Just consider it a tip," Ben said and, turning his back on Fargo's fury, took Bella's arm and guided her inside.

Chapter Six
UNEXPECTED

Long after Ben had left Thief River—all during that homeward ride, he thought about that scene with Fargo, somberly regretting it. There were several reasons for this feeling, but mainly Ben regretted the scene because it told so plainly how far Mace had swung from balance—how little Ben's influence had weighed with him. It had been a last chance to save Mace Fargo from himself and Ben had lost it.

Ever since their kid days, Ben had tried to be a brother to the orphaned Five Diamonds boss. He had found much good in Mace, much to be commended, much that would have been admirable had he but succeeded in bringing it to the fore. He must acknowledge now that all these efforts had been futile; that all this time Mace Fargo had been resenting him. That hurt; it wasn't quite as though Ben had been a stranger butting into Mace's affairs. He'd never intended forcing an attention patently unwelcome on the man—but that was what it had amounted to. He could see that now. Many things that in the past had puzzled him were suddenly clear; it was plain his every act, clear on back to the very beginning, had been misinterpreted. There was that wild streak in young Fargo, that brashness inherited from his father and encouraged by his outlaw uncles; a wildness by the years enhanced and wholly compatible with the dogged willfulness built into him by the cumulative forces of that pernicious early environment. That streak had played, and was still playing, its bitter part.

Some ways Ben blamed himself for the things he saw ahead of Mace. He should have gotten closer to the man and kept that vantage instead of letting the years shove them further and further apart. He should have kept away from entanglement with things that, but—damn it! He wasn't Mace Fargo's keeper! Not even his father's last request could make Ben *that*. The only thing . . . Well, too bad he had not questioned sooner what had been back of that odd asking.

He shook his head; a somber gesture that was just a little grim. A sorry business from first to last. It was not so much a condemnation of Mace's folly that he felt, as pity. Conflicting forces tugged the man. The legacy of his blood had trapped him. He was victim, not of others' scorn, but of his own vast pride and dogged self-delusion. Nothing any man might try would swerve him from his purpose or warp his headlong course by faintest fraction from its ultimate and now foreshadowed end.

Fifteen years ago, Fargo's father had been put in jail for rustling, and there had died before his term was up. His uncles, trying to strip a bank, had been shot in the midst of it, loaded down with plunder. The effect of these things clung to Mace. He could not get them out of mind and willfully had shut his eyes against the Western way that takes men at face value, preferring to believe that he was judged without a hearing; seemed like the man's every thought was drugged with the poison of his family's past. One thing Ben knew: From earliest youth Mace had been obsessed by a resentful conviction of his fancied inferiority, and all his adult actions found their source in desperate efforts to climb out of this estate.

Was it because of Bella Hawes? Was she a motive power in Fargo's life? Were some of these fantastic actions intended to convince her that he was, after all, a power to be reckoned with?

One thing was certain: Bella was mixed in this thing someplace. With a growing dismay not unmixed with a little jealously, Ben had watched Mace's efforts to ingratiate himself with the girl. But whether she looked with favor on his suit or not Ben had no means of knowing. He'd said nothing to her of his own hopes; his code refused that right, things being as they were. But Mace Fargo's views were plain. He regarded Bella as personal property and resented every infringement of that status as a deliberate affront. So he must have regarded Ben's appearance with her at that dance tonight; that may have been the basis of Mace's interference. He might—though Ben did not believe this—have had no real interest in Yettem at all.

Ben's ranch was not a large one. The Two Bars had no payroll. Ben was owner, boss and crew. He ran a few cows and horses, sufficient to keep him busy such times as he was home. So it was with something of a shock that, rounding the final turning of Boulder Canyon along about 2 o'clock, he beheld lamp's light streaming from the ranch house and two saddled broncs tied by the porch.

He stopped the roan at once with sudden flexure of his knees and sat there, dubious and silent, narrowed eyes gone hard and vigilant, darkly raking the heavy shadows.

Of course, this *might* be just a visit—a saddle tramp or two turned in for the night where darkness found them, according to rangeland custom. He, or they, might have left that lamp lit to reassure him, to apprise him of their presence and give proof of friendly intent.

Again, it might be something else. Something designed to drag him from his caution, to bring him tearing into the light where ambush lead could drop him. Such things happened. Western history was studded with such incidents, and that history still was making. He was under no illusion: there were men around this country who would like to see him dead.

Even grubline riding range tramps pulled the saddles off their mounts.

He eased his gun from leather; quietly dropped down off his horse.

It was his own house in that quaker grove—though a man might not have guessed it. His course was circumspect and roundabout. It took him through the deeper gloom and gave him completest knowledge of the layout before it took him to the door and then, more filled with bafflement than ever, it was the back door that he chose.

Uncanny! Not a thing was out of place but those strange broncs beside the porch. Those, and the fact that this house, left dark, was lit. No one lurked in the tree-cast shadows. There was nothing missing. The early morn was undisturbed by any alien sound.

More grimly alert than ever, gun ready in his hand, Ben let himself in softly and moved toward the lighted room. A closed door stood between himself and it. Ben opened it suddenly—and stopped.

Chapter Seven

YETTEM LISTENS

Two people held the room. A woman and a girl.

After that first quick, startled cry with which they'd greeted his appearance, there was no sound. The girl—she could not have been more than ten—clung to her mother, frightened, while the woman's eyes, fixed strangely in a kind of puzzled wonder, searched his face. Blue those eyes were—blue as Colorado lupine; and behind their look of bafflement he thought to read some other thing. Constraint or fear; anxiety—perhaps a blending of all three.

She gave the child a hand's protection, Ben saw with quick approval. She was not a frivolous woman. She had a deep capacity for feeling; was feeling deeply now. She had sustained some kind of shock, he guessed; was striving to adjust herself to some actuality not allowed for. Those other things which first had marked her look receded till only the bafflement remained. She spoke then, slowly, huskily: "You—you're not Yettem . . . ?"

"Well, no, ma'am—no. Not hardly. You were expecting to find him here?"

She said with disappointment, "I thought

I should. I—We—That is . . . He's not here, then?"

Ben thought to detect a sudden dread, a kind of grim desperation in her tone. It made him pause. "Did he tell you he would meet you here?"

"Oh, no!" she answered quickly. "He'd no idea we were coming. It was just that—This *is* the Two Bars ranch, isn't it?"

"Yes, ma'am. This is Two Bars," Ben said gravely.

"He hasn't sold it, has he?"

"Yettem?" Ben's eyes narrowed thoughtfully. "No, ma'am. Ace hasn't sold it."

She seemed relieved. The pale cheeks showed a little color now. "I guess you're the foreman, aren't you? I'm Mrs. Yettem. This—" she patted the little girl's shoulder, "is our daughter, Raechel. How long do you expect Mr. Yettem to be gone? Is he on a cattle-buying trip or something?"

"Why, yes, ma'am; I expect he is. No tellin' when he will be gettin' back. Sometimes," Ben said a little drily, "he goes as much as two hundred miles when the cattle-buyin' mood gets hold of him. You say he wasn't expectin' you?"

"Well, not just yet, that is. He wrote last month that he'd be sending for us soon now—we've been living at Independence—you know, Missouri. It gets pretty lonesome living away off that way. Except for a few infrequent visits, we haven't seen Ace for more than ten years." She looked down into her hands; work-reddened hands they were that told Ben quite a lot. Then she was looking up at him suddenly with moisture in her eyes; with other things staring from them that made Ben look away.

She said: "He's worked so hard—slaving all these years to build a home for us. When he wrote last month saying things were nearly ready, I—we just couldn't wait any longer. We decided to surprise him."

Yettem would be surprised all right, Ben thought.

He said: "You came in by Thief River, I expect, ma'am, didn't you? Took the stage at—"

"No. We came from Sleepy Cat—"

"Mean to say that you an' this little girl rode all the way from Sleepy Cat a-horseback?" He couldn't seem to believe it. "Why, that's more than forty miles, ma'am!"

"Is it that far?" She smiled tiredly; and the child stared at him from wide blue eyes that *did* kind of look like Yettem's, except that hers were young and wide and innocent, whereas Yettem's were always squinting and filled with maliciousness or guile. "Well, it was worth it," the mother said. "We didn't have a single stopover coming this way. And if you'd been away from your husband long as I have . . ."

Ben nodded. "I guess that's so. Well, you two

better be turnin' in, ma'am. No point your waitin' up any longer. Hard tellin' when Ace'll be gettin' back—be several days yet, anyway. Just make yourselves at home. There's grub an' stuff in the kitchen cupboards. Anything else you need, just holler. I'll be sayin' good night now, ma'am."

"Good night," they said, and Ben closed the door behind him.

Mace Fargo had broken with Taylor in the overpowering anger roused by seeing him there with Bella. Resentment had spurred him into seizing Yettem's plight as excuse. It had been a mistake—a bad mistake. He saw that clearly as he joined the cursing Yettem two miles south of Tortilla Flat. He glared at Yettem, face distorted in the yellow glow from the dashboard. "Fine fizzle you made of things—"

"I'll get that bustard yet," breathed Yettem wickedly. "Mark my words, boy. One of these days they'll be findin' that guy with his guts spewed out!"

But Fargo wasn't listening. He was recalling, thus belatedly, his need for keeping Taylor friendly. Instead of which, in a fit of temper egged on by his deviling jealousy, he had broken with the man; broken finally, irretrievably. It was bitter knowledge; the more so in that, save for his pride, he might have patched things up.

Worse than this, though, had been his coming

out in front of all Thief River as Yettem's champion. Yettem, the suspected cow thief. That was bad. Acknowledged friendship with such a man could hardly be called an asset.

He stopped the car on a sudden impulse. "Here's where I'm leavin' you," he told Yettem.

"Huh?" The man raked a look at the moonlit desolation 'round about. "Leavin' me? What the hell you talkin' about, boy?"

"Just that. Leavin' you. This is where you get out."

"Nuts. Get goin'. You can leave me out by—"

"I'm leavin' you here. Hop out."

Yettem looked at him. "Ha, ha," he said. "Very funny. Now get this crock to rollin' an' let's get down to the ranch. I got—"

Fargo's hand came out of the door pocket. "Are you gettin' out?"

Yettem's eyes were gleaming slits above the sunburn of his cheeks. "What the hell you tryin' to pull? You fixin' to throw me over?" The words were low, barely above a whisper; smooth and hard as a knife blade rubbed on velvet. "Listen to me, boy—"

Fargo's shoulders moved impatiently. " 'Course I ain't throwin' you over. Blood's thicker'n water, ain't it? Then quit bein' an ass. That was a damn-fool stunt I pulled, backin' you in public like I did tonight. We've got to watch ourselves. Can't afford to be seen—"

"That's right . . ." The scowl dropped off of Yettem's cheeks. "Holy cats! D'you suppose—?"

"Can't tell. We'll know tomorrow, like enough. Choke off the blat now an' get out before somebody comes along an' spots us. Well? What you waitin' on?"

"I just thought of somethin'—"

Fargo snorted. "I'll do all the thinking necessary —"

Yettem leered. "Your ol' man said that to me once. Damn near got me swung with his thinkin'. Seems to me like I oughta have some kind of guarantee—"

"I'll guarantee you in a minute!"

"All right. I'm gettin' out. But Christ, boy! You think I'm goin' to walk—"

"Thurman's place is just over the rise. You can walk that far, I guess."

"I wish the hell you'd—"

"Goddamn it!" Fargo swore. "Get out before I throw you out!" He watched impatiently while Yettem sullenly climbed from the car. "You can tell Thurman your horse stepped in a dog hole. Tell him anything you like. He'll give you a horse—there ain't a rancher in this country would dare refuse you. Get hold of your crowd an' get busy. An' look—change the play for tomorrow night to Hockaday. I'm havin' his bunch come over to a meetin'—"

"Good God, Mace! Hockaday's—"

"Do what I tell you!" Fargo said and slammed the door. A moment later, he was roaring off with the button flat to the floorboards.

Chapter Eight
OUT OF THE PAST

It was early morning of the day following the dance, with a bright sun splashing all that greenrock waste and gilding thorny chaparral with dapples of light like lacquer, when Holders Hockaday came riding into Mad Spring and racked his horse before its solitary structure, Kate Stalleon's paintless, sprawling roadhouse.

"Madame up?" he asked the Portuguese swamper.

The man pointed at a far door labeled "PRIVATE" and with a grunt the Three Rings owner clanked his spurs across the place, pushing into the room beyond without the formality of knocking.

A big and rawboned woman sat dunking doughnuts in her coffee at a Louis XIV table. A mop of hair—once brilliantly yellow as the gold taken out of Thief River—hung about her bony shoulders and gave her a witch-like look strongly emphasized by sunken cheeks and a toothless, red-gummed grin.

"I see the years ain't improved your manners none."

Hockaday brusquely waved that aside. His look softened a little then and he said slowly: "Bad news, Kate. Mace has broken with Taylor—last night at Tortilla schoolhouse. Right in front of everybody."

"You've got to warn him, Holders—"

"It's a little late for that," said Hockaday grimly. "That goddamn Yettem was trying his luck with Ben again. Ben knocked him down and Mace came rushing up in a lather. He said, 'Don't lay your hand on him again.'"

Kate Stalleon sat a long time staring at her jeweled fingers. When her eyes came up they were very dark and her cheeks were white behind the paint dabbed on them. "You've got to stop it, Holders," she said huskily. "You've *got* to. We—"

He shook his handsome head. "No one but God can stop it now. Taylor questioned his interest in Yettem an' Mace told him to mind his own business. He said: 'You play your hand and I'll play mine,' and quick as a flash Ben said, 'You better watch where that hand is taking you.'"

Kate Stalleon said, "My God!" and her hands gripped the table tightly.

Once more Hockaday's head shook regretfully. "I hated to come here with this, Kate, but I thought you'd want to know." It was odd the way he looked at that disreputable old woman. But there'd been a time when any man in the Superstitions would have given a right leg gladly for her favors, and some of them still remembered. Holders Hockaday was one.

She said slowly, "Yettem always was a wild

one, but I had hoped—" She broke off to stare at him, startled. "Do you suppose Mace knows—?"

Hockaday put a thoughtful hand to his mustache. "Hard tellin'," he remarked at last. "But where would he be findin' it out at this late date? All the old crowd is dead an' gone. All but you an' me—Say! What about Reb Fargo? He'd know, wouldn't he?"

"Reb? He was just a kid when Mace was born. Hell," she said, "he was only eight years old! An' he ain't around now anyway."

She put her elbows on the table, ground bony fists against her cheeks.

"Didn't Fargo know?"

Madame snorted. "Fork Fargo didn't even know enough to button his pants up when he was finished," she said contemptuously. "Mace never found it out from *him*."

The silence stretched awhile then Hockaday murmured, "How come you an' old Taylor never got hitched after his wife died?"

The old look flashed in her eyes for a moment; flashed briefly and as swiftly died. "We were kind of scared, I guess. The conventions kind of bothered some of us those days, Holders." She shrugged, and then her cheeks went pale again as she remembered what had brought the Three Rings owner here. She cried: "What has Mace been up to, Holders?"

"Been hatchin' a little ambition, looks like.

Got a bee in his bonnet. I reckon he wants more range, for one thing—"

"I mean how'd he come to take up for Yettem that way? Is the man an entire *fool?* Don't he know the kind of rep Ace Yettem's got? Don't he know what folks'll think?"

"Mebbe he don't give a damn," said Hockaday. "Some ways, Kate, Mace is pretty damn bullheaded." Looking at her that way, a faint smile tugged his lips. He said then, wholly serious: "Someone got off with a good-sized jag of Mace's beef last week. At the dance last night Yettem accused Ben of it—"

"And Ben let him get away with it?"

"He didn't do a great deal about it—"

"He let Yettem call him a rustler in front of that crowd and didn't kill him?" Kate Stalleon said incredulously. Her cheeks showed color enough right then, Hockaday noticed with a twinge.

He said: "Well, it wasn't quite like that. Taylor tried to make it sound ridiculous. But Yettem said the stuff was on his ranch—"

"Then the stuff was planted!" Madame cried. "God damn it, Holders—can't you *see* it? They're tryin' to frame him!"

Hockaday sighed a little, put that smoothing hand across his mustache. "I wonder . . ." he said oddly. "You know, Taylor's not been much in evidence 'round here lately. Lots of folks been wonderin' why. Where d'you s'pose he's been goin' to? There's a lot of room for truth in what Yettem claims. Ide tried his hand at trailin', a little spell back, and he tracked Ben far as Sawik Mountain. What's—"

"He didn't track any cattle up there, did he?"

"That don't signify, Kate, an' you know it. If Taylor's lifting cattle an' sellin' 'em to those Salt River Indians—"

"Have you gone crazy? Is that what Yettem claims?" she demanded scathingly.

"Well, I don't know that he claims it; but the idea's driftin' 'round. After all nobody *knows* what Taylor's doing—"

"My God! To think all these years I been givin' you credit for a little sense. You listen to me, Holders Hockaday. There's not a single crooked tissue in that boy's makeup!"

The boss of Three Rings smiled a little sadly. "You sure were gone on Jack—"

"Jack Taylor was the straightest man in this whole country, Holders—and don't you ever doubt it! He was a damn good marshal, too, and—"

"But I notice he kept his mouth shut about—"

"It was my wish made him do it!"

Hockaday shrugged. "Have it your way," he said. "But that don't—" He stopped abruptly, scowled and rasped a considering hand across his chin. He looked at her sharply. "How old was Mace when Reb Fargo run away?"

She returned his stare, head canted. She

said thoughtfully: "It must be around twenty-five years now since the day Reb knifed Judge Houghton and ducked for the timber. That's a long time, Holders; a long, long time . . ."

"How old was Mace?" reminded Hockaday, sticking to the subject.

Madame's brows revealed the years' furrows as she turned it over in her mind. "Let's see . . . Reb's been gone a good twenty-five years. He was twelve when he run off. Mace was—I mean *Reb* was eight years old when Mace was born. That would make Mace four when—"

"Four, eh?" Hockaday interrupted. "D'you remember what Reb looked like? Did he look much like old Fork?"

"Wait," she said. "I got a picture 'round here someplace—one of those daguerreo things. Hold on. I'll see if I can find it."

Hockaday watched her go to an old trunk over in the room's far corner; watched her rummage through the musty clothes and faded keepsakes of her past. He saw a jeweled fan he once had given her, the satin between its ribs now brittle and torn. Then she was coming back, extending a little tintype.

He took it, studied it, frowning; peered closer and suddenly nodded. He laid the picture on the table. He said: "Know what I think? I think, by God, Reb Fargo's back here—I think he's been back quite a spell!"

Madame said "Nerts!" inelegantly. "D'you think I wouldn't have known him if he was?"

He said with conviction: "Reb Fargo's here—he's the bird we know as Yettem!"

Chapter Nine

AMMUNITION FOR HOTHEADS

Taylor had discerned at least one truth: Mace Fargo had got ambition.

When Ben's old man had sent Fork Fargo over the road, Five Diamonds had been a valued, going concern; it was but a husk, a gutted ranch, when Mace came into it, its worthwhile stock driven off to redeem Fork Fargo's trespasses. The boy had cursed for days, his soul gone bitter-black with hate; he had cursed Fork Fargo up and down, cursed God and everybody else who might conceivably have had a hand in stripping him of his heritage. Then, brooding, seething with resentment, he had gone off into the hills. Save for a quieter mien, when he returned months later he was to all outward seeming the same wild youth who'd gone storming off; he had the same tousled, unruly yellow hair, the same rebellious eyes.

The changes—not at once apparent—were of the soul and of the mind. The boy who left the gutted ranch and the man who finally came back to it were as fundamentally different as night from day. In the solitude of wind-swept places a new entity had been forged from the ashes of the old. This was a man to be reckoned with. A youth as burly, yellow-haired and dark of eye as ever, but a man endowed with each stark quality of his background and environment. A haunted man, hounded by the shame that others had put upon him, by the fancied low opinion of his neighbors, and by a lust for success that naught but death could ever quench.

The inherited tendencies were there. That recklessness of temper still rode with him, but there was caution added. Incompatible qualities? Not at all—not when fused, by subtlety, by sharp discernment, hate and a crafty, sly, designing nature. Mace had all these in plenty; they were a part, an untakable part, of his heritage. He knew what he wanted now, knew what he meant to have—and saw how to go about getting it.

Mace Fargo wanted power.

He knew the way to power was fear. Hadn't Fork Fargo done very nicely until they made Jack Taylor sheriff? Taylor, the man who couldn't be bought? Very well; before Mace got through, Fork Fargo would look like a piker. Jack Taylor was dead and gone now. Young Ben was a different sort; he hadn't his father's toughness—he let considerations sway him. No considerations should sway Mace Fargo, damn them! This mountain country was ideal land for a cattle kingdom. It needed but one little thing—

consolidation: One man to stand at the head of things, to give the orders, to lay down the law for the rest—one man to gobble its profits.

That man was going to be Mace Fargo.

An ambitious project, certainly. One that few could hope to realize in a life's span. But ambition was the key to Mace's new character; it was his governing impulse, his reason for existence. Here was this Thief River country, a cattle empire lying dormant, steadily and ever more swiftly going to seed under the misguided applications of the unimaginative, past-bound flotsam that controlled it. Shorn of scruples, Fargo saw in this a situation ready-made for his new passion; saw his chance for conquest, for building his Five Diamonds far beyond its former glory—saw this chance and took it.

He set about the task by easy stages. By industry and perseverance he built his outfit up until the payroll numbered three times seven hands. His cattle roved the mountain meadows. He leased forest lands for additional pasturage and, in time, bought out a number of smaller owners, throwing their brands in with his own, gradually absorbing them. His horseflesh with passing years became second only to the beasts of Jesse Hawes in quality.

It was when things had reached this point that the depredations of rustlers began definitely to worry the Thief River country. Stealing of cattle and horses had always been more or less common in the section; but it had been sporadic stealing, controlled theft that had greatly bothered no one. Now it was like an epidemic, hitting ranchers from the Salt River clear down into the Superstitions. Hitting them hard. Cattle and horseflesh simply vanished. Nothing was left behind to show a clue to the takers' identity. Very seldom could any rancher say with assurance just where or when they'd been stolen; all that was known were that they had gone.

Day and night the Association was hounded with bitter recriminations. Why didn't they do something? Why didn't they stop it? What the hell were folks paying in dues for? But the Association appeared helpless, as much in the dark as its individual members. Then one day a sheriff rode into Thief River with a warrant for Abe Peyrolles; he was taken out and hanged. In swift succession disaster struck down Birchman, Galloway, Bucks Younger. The county seethed with rumor. Men's passions broke and flared beyond the reach of sanity—flared red as the flames of cabins burned down in the dead of night. There was no safety. Security was an abstract feeling dragged from the past like something remembered from a dream. No man dared trust his neighbors, for no man knew which was crook and which was lawman.

Onto this stage set for Death rode Mace

Fargo with his plan for ridding Thief River of thieves.

That first meeting of the country's ranchers called by Fargo at Five Diamonds—the meeting Taylor had refused to join—showed local history in the making. There were no startling or secret developments, nothing which a spy, had there been one present, could later have revealed to adverse interests. One thing only marked its importance: Fargo's plan was adopted. Fargo said: "We've got to meet brute force with brute force. We're goin' to run these goddamn thieves clean out of the country! There ain't two ways about it; there's the hounds—that's us—an' the foxes. Those that won't run with the hounds we got to figure with the foxes. That's right, ain't it?" And the attending ranchers stood behind him to a man.

Fargo had not overlooked the advantage of political backing in his cleanup. The next meeting, held the night following that epoch-marking dance at Tortilla schoolhouse, showed a bigger turnout; there were new folks come from the outlying ranches—reinforcements from the remoter settlements, and among them was Sheriff Bett Tanter. Fargo had gotten in touch with him the afternoon before and in a long and confidential talk had proved to Tanter where the sheriff's bread could best be buttered. Tanter was a cautious man, a plodder. He didn't like these extra-legal methods. What if the damn thing backfired? Why, God damn it, they'd have his hide on the fence! But in the end Fargo talked him over.

"What this country needs," Fargo said, "is a cleanup that'll make it safe for women and children. Way things are with all these potshootin' desperadoes driftin' 'round, a man takes his life in his hands every time he opens his door. Too many strangers ridin' through these hills—too damned much infernal rustling goin' on. We got to stop it. Sheer matter of self-defense! Last week I lost a hundred an' seventy-eight steers! Where the hell will you an' I be if this keeps up many more weeks? I tell you, Tanter, we got to act—got to strike while the iron's hot!"

So the sheriff had come and was noted with relief by numbers of those others who had gathered before Five Diamonds ranch house. Fargo did the talking, casually roping Tanter in whenever a point needed clinching. He said the goddam thieves had practically taken the country over. That the sheriff, hard as everyone knew he had been working, had finally admitted he was unable to cope with the situation, had asked their help. The county funds, he said, already had been heavily overdrawn in the procurement of posses and additional emergency deputies. That the time had come when every able-bodied honest rancher ought to be willing to serve in the furtherment of law and order without expectation of monetary reward. Their interests, their homes, their very *lives* depended on it. The sheriff, he said, had reached the reluctant conclusion that only by the organization of a citizens' committee could the forces of anarchy and sedition effectively be put down. Thievery, he declared, had reached the heights of traditional business; stealing had become an institution, and unless they banded themselves together in a solid front behind the law, the cattle business, as represented in this county, had seen its finish.

"Let's show Tanter we're behind him," he concluded. "All in favor holler 'Aye.' "

The mighty shout that rose on the instant shook the veranda floorboards. Fargo turned with the air of one presenting a laurel wreath and beckoned Tanter up beside him on the porch. He smiled and clapped the sheriff on the back. "Guess that ought to show you, Bettman, how us Thieve River ranchers feel on the subject. You've got this crowd behind you to a man."

Tanter licked his lips. The smile he put across them lacked considerable of being robust. He would like to have pointed out that the idea wasn't his in the first place; that he wasn't asking for this demonstration or for this backing—that he'd prefer to go on doing things as he had been. But he lacked the moral fiber. He'd been put out on a limb and the limb was creaking, creaking badly. He was scared to go any farther and, with Fargo's eyes upon him, he hadn't the nerve to crawl back.

Fargo addressed the crowd. "Since this is, in effect then, a citizens' committee, we've got to draft some man for executive. Somebody's got to lead us. Nominations are in order."

The sheriff's name was mentioned. Hockaday said tentatively: "What about Ben Taylor?" Growls and considerable muttering broke out and half a score of heads looked around at the Three Rings owner unpleasantly. Hockaday sat back down in his wagon-seat and thereafter kept his mouth shut.

Kreel, the Five Diamonds foreman, got up then and said it looked like there was only one man in the gathering who'd be capable of the task—Mace Fargo; and Fargo was voted in.

He called Tanter to stand beside him at the veranda rail. With a hand thrown comradely fashion across Bett Tanter's shoulders, he addressed the crowd. "Our object in forming this law-and-order association is to help the sheriff rid this county of crooks—especially rustlers and the floating riffraff driven in from other places. If there's anything about our program that's not compatible to the smooth and effective furtherance of duly constituted law I'm expecting the sheriff to come out and say so. We want the law behind us, not against us."

He made a magnetic, persuasive figure as he stood there by the sheriff with the cool wind roughing up his yellow hair. His burly shape breathed confidence, efficiency; his bluff and sometimes-smiling features reassured the more timid in the gathering, and those who did not agree entirely with him put their faith in the sheriff's presence and threw off their worried doubtings in the imagined sanction of elected law.

"The first step then," Fargo told them, "is to find out what's going on. I suggest we set some men to watching the trails at night. It's essential that we know who's movin' about, who's travelin' these hills after dark comes. Somebody has suggested the most of our cattle are bein' stole in daylight; mebbe a lot of 'em are, but there's a damned sight more goin' out of here after nightfall. If they're goin' by truck, a watch on the roads'll stop 'em. Now, Mose Crowley's agreed to keep an eye on the Goldfield road. Monk Ide's goin' to take Horse Mesa. I'll watch the trails cuttin' northwest towards Salt River. How about you, Hockaday, seein' to that Castle Dome road? You'll do that? Fine!" One after another, he sounded the larger ranchers and sent them off to watch some special stretch of country. When that much was settled he said: "Every outgoin' truck you see, stop it. I want to know what's carried—"

"Hell, you can't do that," objected Hockaday. "Plenty of honest men are sendin' out cattle by truck—"

"If a man and his load are honest, they lose nothing by being stopped. It's the only way we can lick this goddamn rustling, Holders. We've got to check every steer taken out." He looked at the sheriff. Tanter nodded.

"Some of these boys ain't goin' to like it," Ham Meeker muttered. "There's a lot of ranches scattered 'round this country that ain't got no rep at this meetin'—"

"They were told about it. If they don't want part in it, they've got a reason. There's just two sides in this business—hounds an' foxes. Outfits represented in this committee are the hounds—"

"I think," Hockaday said, "I'll get out of it."

"You have that privilege," Fargo answered. "If you want to be classed with the foxes, that's your lookout. I'll say this to you: a wise man stays on the side of the law."

"What law?" said Hockaday, bridling. "The kind that comes out of a gun-barrel?"

Fargo smiled drily. "There'll be gunpowder burned—make no mistake about that. Use your head a minute, Holders. This situation's drastic; drastic measures will have to be taken to effect a cure. You can't fight fire with confetti! Give these crooks a good strong taste of what we've got in store and you've got the thing half licked.

There'll not be many have the guts to buck us. They'll cut stick an' run—"

"What about the little guys? What about the nesters?"

"Well, what *is* a nester?" Fargo asked. "A shiftless sort at best. Mostly he's a range tramp; a guy who's come driftin' in from God knows where an' squatted on a hunk of some big outfit's range. If the big guy's an easy mark, he lets him stay awhile, figurin' the weather'll solve the problem for him. But sometimes it don't. The nester sticks. Sometimes he gets to be a two-bit cowman—but *how?* Nine times out of ten he gets his start through rustlin' the big guy's cattle. You know that well as I do! Where's there any percentage helpin' that kind of maverick? I—"

"How'd you get *your* start?" asked Hockaday.

"By damn hard work an' plenty of it—as anyone can tell you! *You* ought to know; plenty's the time I've taken forty a month an' found for punchin' your stuff 'round the country. But we didn't come here to listen to any Alger stories about me—we came to do a job of work, an' I don't blame the sheriff losin' his patience waitin' for us to get at it. If you ain't figurin' to watch the Castle Dome road for us, say so an' I'll give the job to somebody else."

"Well, I'll watch it," Hockaday said, but his tone was far from hearty. "I'll watch it an' I'll stop the trucks, but—"

"That's all we're askin' of you," Fargo said; and turned his attention elsewhere. "What was that you was askin', Meeker?"

"I been wonderin' what we're supposed to do if any of these trucks don't stop. Some of them mightn't want to consider—"

"They'll consider a gun!" snapped Fargo hotly. "Get this through your heads, men. We're tryin' to stop this goddamn stealin', an' halfway measures ain't goin' to work. If a man shows fight, it shows he's crooked. Open up—shoot first an' do your jawin' after!"

Meeker said: "That's a dangerous—"

"It's meant to be!" Fargo barked roughly. "The only way to deal with crooks is feed 'em the fear of God!" He shoved a hard stare around belligerently. "I hear there's been some talk about my takin' up for Yettem—about what I had to say to Taylor last night. If there's anyone 'round here'd like to learn more about it, now's the time to open his face." He sloshed his glance around promiscuously. "There ain't, eh? Then I guess that's all for tonight."

Chapter Ten
GRIM PORTENT

The arrival of Yettem's wife and child at Two Bars would, under any circumstance, have proved embarrassing to Taylor; coming at the time it did, their visit was a catastrophe of the gravest order. Now, more than anywhere in memory, he had need of a rein unqualifiedly free. He needed the liberty to think and act without regard for others. That liberty was denied him by these people's presence.

Night had come again, reminding him of lost time sorely needed; had come and caught him with a mind still undecided how to deal with this new responsibility a harrowing fate had thrust upon him. Had he told them the truth at once, the situation might have resolved itself; no matter how tearfully, the woman would have gone. But he had concealed the truth. The innate chivalry of him had balked before the prospect of dealing the woman's blind faith such a crushing blow. He'd not paused to reflect that, bitter as it was, the truth must out—that all his evasion could give her was, at best, but a moment's respite.

He should be riding; should have left, in fact,

long since. The need was urgent. There were things that had to be done—that could not be put off.

Yet he had put them off.

All day he'd lain with a rifle, screened by brush, atop the rimrock. With strained eyes red rimmed, slitted, he had watched the Two Bars buildings— watched with his finger curled around steel. Had riders come he would have shot them, knowing well the single purpose which could bring them to his ranch. One rider *had* come, finally. Late in the afternoon it was, and Taylor's eyes went grim and hard as he recognized the lank, big, bony shape of old Kate Stalleon. Even in the blackness of his mood—in the desperate despair with which he waited out this vigil, he found time to wonder what had brought her. He'd watched her briefly talking with Yettem's wife; watched her drearily riding off.

At dusk he had come down for supper and eaten in brooding silence the cold snack given him by Yettem's wife; had parried absently her questions about her husband and had hardly seemed to be listening when she spoke of the woman's visit. "She asked for you—your name *is* Taylor, isn't it? Well, she wouldn't tell me what she wanted. I said I guessed you were out with the men someplace. She looked at me kind of queer, I thought; but she didn't say anything. Just grunted and rode off. Have you any idea who she was?"

"I reckon. Friend of my father's," he'd said briefly.

Now, sitting with the rifle close beside him in the doorway of the harness shed, he peered off into the darkening canyon and thought about the bitter pranks of which a careless fate was capable. Ironic and unpalatable as were these musings, he bleakly faced the facts. His purpose in returning at this time to Thief River—hazardous enough at best—was like to be defeated by so small a thing as this inopportune arrival of two wholly inconsequential people—the abandoned wife and child of a cattle thief it was entirely in the cards he might have to kill.

This woman and this girl, sublimely unconscious of their momentary importance, mattered when weighed against the things at stake no more than the spatter of a single raindrop. Yet, despite this fact, they were people, fellow humans, entitled to his consideration; and his heart rebelled at thought of letting them pay the price of their unwitting blunder. It was Yettem who should pay—Yettem, who had made them think he owned this Two Bars ranch.

If only he had a crew—had just one man, thought Taylor bitterly. Or if Steve Fontana would come dropping by. Someone—anyone that could take their responsibility off his hands so he could ride!

God damn this chicken-heartedness! What

were these people to him that he should shirk his business to take care of them? He should be riding; should have been gone from here long since. He had his part to play. The board was set, the pawns were moving and the evil of their brewing hung above this high hill country like a dark miasma—like a blanket loomed in hell and shaken for the devil's laughter.

He had to grit his teeth when he thought of Fargo—of Mace sitting back, secure, like some great spider in the web of his duplicity. Mace was like that, like a spider, weaving, weaving, running his hairy paws across men's hopes, beliefs, and hatreds; snaring them in his gleaming mesh of lies and little caring what became of them, what suffering, what agony might be their portion, just so he sat the uncrowned king of all this wasteland empire.

The man was mad to think he could encompass it. Was mad and damned—was doubly damned with the infamy of that vile alliance by which he sought to gain his ends.

Just thinking about it this way made Ben Taylor's hackles rise. Ben's dad had said, "Look out for him"—and this was what had come of it.

In the thickening shadows of the harness shed Ben's mind went back to that far day. He saw that upstairs room in the old hotel; recalled the pattern of its orchid paper, the faded carpet on the floor, the great four-poster where his father lay burnt up with fever; recalled the queer, bright look of the old man's sunken eyes. He felt again the old man's grip, the startling, urgent pressure of those hot and bony fingers. "Keep an eye on the boy, Ben, won't you? I'd hate to see him wind up like the rest of that tribe—like his uncles or young Reb, or the way Fork Fargo has." And Ben had promised, not understanding, but out of kindness, in the hope of bringing comfort to a dying man.

Even yet he did not understand it clearly. But of late dark fancies had begun to stir, and it was these that put those bleak, tight lines about his mouth. These and thoughts of what Mace had put his hand to.

It wasn't so much that Fargo had got to running with the wrong kind of hombres, for he hadn't been in the habit of running with any kind. He was like Ben that way; a lone-wolf sort of fellow. Mace liked to fancy himself a leader and, of late, was exhibiting many indications of intending to be one. This lust for leadership, this desire to be at the head of things had often, Ben reflected, gotten Fargo mixed up in escapades showing little credit to his judgment. But Mace always had been brash. There was an impetuosity in his character that had seldom known the restraining influence either of public opinion or thought of possible consequence. What Mace had wanted he had gone belligerently after and, more often than not, had gotten it. He was after something now, characteristically full tilt.

And yet, as Ben had always contended, there were many admirable things about young Fargo. He was generous to a fault, and if he liked a man, would back him to the limit. He had a cold, hard courage and was dogged in his tenacity. He had vision. An opportunist, his grasp of circumstance was nothing short of remarkable. In themselves these were sterling qualities. In Mace they were dangerous weapons; and he'd found a way to use them.

It was his name, Ben guessed, that hurt Mace most. It had made the man a rebel. Even as a child there'd been that consciousness of liability in the way that he had used it; there'd been that resentful tone of voice, that hard belligerence in his stare. It was like a plague upon him—like an incubus; its grip had tightened with each passing year. It was a lash to Mace's ambition, a mainspring for his ego.

It was, perhaps, Fargo's certainty of social ostracism that had made him take up Yettem. Their acquaintanceship had started over pistols. Guns had been abhorrent to Mace Fargo as a boy. When the Five Diamonds came to him, he'd thrown every firearm into the nearest creek, and not again—until a year ago—had he so much as put his hand on one. Then, strangely, one windy day last fall he'd come to town and bought one;

the best that money could buy. He said in a joking way he'd decided to learn to shoot, and Yettem, lounging at the store, had volunteered to teach him.

From that time their acquaintance dated; and it had been with considerable misgivings that Ben had watched it grow. More and more, he thought, Mace had fallen under the gunman's influence, until today he was actively directing that very group which, publicly, he had sworn he would destroy.

The sound of drumming hoofs roused Taylor from his brooding. Quick it was, and frantic, pouring up the canyon like a prelude to approaching doom. He came to his feet, bleak-eyed and grim, rifle cuddled—ready.

A lone horse's shape tore around the bend, streaked straight for the Two Bars' buildings. With a muttered oath Taylor dropped his gun, hurrying forward into the shadows. A startled gasp came from Yettem's wife as he sprang, caught the mustang's bridle and was dragged twenty fighting feet with his whole weight braked in his bootheels before he pulled the beast to a stop. A still shape hung from the saddle—battered, but still lashed fast; and Taylor needed no light to tell him whose it was or from whom it came.

The Winds of Destiny were blowing. There were things a man couldn't shirk.

Chapter Eleven
SHOCK

Because he was chicken-hearted, for the sake of this woman and her child, Ben Taylor had sent the last thin edge of his advantage packing, had turned his back on Fortune, and let Big Mace play host to Opportunity. He had known hours earlier what this night must hold in store for some large rancher. He had known it from the man who now hung stark in death from this scratched saddle; had seen, days back, how Fargo's hand depended for its strength not alone in waging war on rustlers, but on turning, as well, one set of ranchmen against another—big owners against the small. Only by this could the man ever hope to achieve his purpose. All the misery, heartbreak and agony that must dog his path to empire were as nothing to big Mace Fargo. Pillage and ambush and arson would ride the vanguard to his victory; battle, death and swift oblivion would crowd their heels till Thief River's creeks ran red with blood and all this high hill country was thrown to the wolves of chaos.

A terrible price to pay, perhaps, for title to empty acres. But what cared Fargo? *He'd* not pay! This kingdom would be bought with the lives of others; with the lives of men turned blind with bitter hatred by his lies, with the lives of those whose suspicions made of them easy victims—with the lives of the fools who listened to his hints of easy booty. Fools flocked to a get-rich system like flies to a sorghum barrel. And when it was over, leaving Fargo in the saddle, who would dare complain?

Taylor had foreseen all this—had even guessed that Hockaday would be the man picked first to fall and speed the avalanche on its way. Ben had aimed to warn him, but the coming of Yettem's kin had forced his hand. The knowledge he had dug from those long weeks of riding had chained him here with this woman and girl. He cursed again that soft streak in his nature. But he could not go, leaving Yettem's wife and child to face alone the expected arrival of Yettem's raiders.

For that they would come Taylor had no doubt. They would have learned by now—indeed this still shape's fate proved that they *had* learned—the secret back of his long absences. Retaliation had been, as he had seen it, but a matter of hours, perhaps of minutes; that it had not come thus far was but a jest of sardonic fate.

Retaliation would come; Yettem's pack would be wild to get his scalp. Their vengeance would not be withheld from his buildings nor, in his absence, from anyone found therein. That had been why he could not go leaving the girl and her mother alone here. By the time recognition reached Yettem, their shameful fate would have been sealed. Might have been sealed, even, anyway; their history showed the depth of Yettem's interest.

Taylor's desire had been to protect these people also from the truth of Yettem's status; otherwise he'd have sent them long since to some place of greater security and thus been rid of them—left free to act. But he must bundle them off from here now whether they learned the truth or not. He would send them with a note to Kate—to Kate Stalleon, his father's friend. She could do that much for him.

He cut the dead man's lashings, gently easing him to the ground. This was Jansen—old Nels Jansen, the operative furnished by the local Association. A good man, too. A sight too good for such an end as this.

Taylor looked away, staring bleakly off through the shadows; staring past the white-faced woman, the muscles knotted along his jaw. They'd pay for this. He swore it.

In the meantime Hockaday's Three Rings was gone, demolished, a gutted mockery to the hopes of honest ranching, reduced by now to scattered stumps, to charred, still-smoking ashes. Jansen's fate admitted no other reasoning. Ben had sent the man to Hockaday's that morning, had equipped him with a pair of glasses and a few curt words of advice.

And now the man was dead.

A bitter jibe, their sending him back this way; a jibe, grim taunt, a challenge—a challenge that had to be answered.

The woman had got past his guard, had seen the crumpled thing that lay in the sand by his feet. Her choking sobs made a piteous sound and he put a comforting arm about her, let her cry against his chest.

Doom hovered above the treetops, lurked in the dark, hushed shadows and crouched in the gurgle of each stream. Ben had cut his string too short and the time had come to pay.

Jesse Hawes, keeper of the corral at Thief River Crossing, had come home from Fargo's meeting in an odd, dour kind of satisfaction. It showed in the malicious gleaming of his eyes, in the way his teeth clamped down on his tobacco, in the lean condescending smile with which he greeted Bella. She watched him throw his hat in a corner, hitch up his creaky rocker and prop his feet on the table. He sat back then and watched her, something avid in the intent regard of the hard gray eyes beneath his heavy brows. It were as though he'd predicted the fall of Rome and with his own eyes had beheld it burning.

"Well, what's happened?" she asked finally. "What's got you all stirred up so?"

"They burned Three Rings to the ground tonight. Hamstrung Holders' best saddlers, cut his fences, killed over half his stock an' drove off what was left of it. Killed three men, too. And—"

"They?" cried Bella, startled. "Who do you mean—?"

"Bunch of small-spread cowmen—they've all thrown in with the rustlers. Bunch of goddam riffraff, just like Fargo says. Hockaday's wild as a hatter. We got the news just before the meetin' broke up. Sheriff's organized him a posse an' gone off hot on the trail—probably lynch every one of 'em. An' serve 'em damn well right! What's more—"

"But do they know who did it? I don't see—"

"They know, all right. Most of Hockaday's bunch came with him. But he left five men to watch the spread an' kind of keep an eye on his beef stuff—had 'em gathered, you know, for shippin'. Well, two of those boys got away; they come larrupin' with the news. Liked to killed their horses gettin' there, but they made it. Recognized four five of the raiders—Klings an' Reed an' Walston; one or two of them other fellers from over 'round Fish Creek Mountain. An' Monk Ide says he seen Ben Taylor with 'em!"

Bella stared at him with cheeks gone white as parchment.

"Told you that damn young Taylor was a maverick," he said, "an' I guess this proves it. Ide says he saw him with a torch in his hand settin' fire to Hockaday's haystacks. Infernal whelp! I told you to keep away from him. Mebbe this'll teach you to—"

"It's a lie!" she flared. "A dirty, vicious lie—and I know why they told it! How could Ide—"

"He was over there, an' it ain't no lie. Ide was over there seein' that cousin of his about somethin'. Curly Langtry—one of the fellers that got killed. Ide's a little tough, I guess, but I'd take his word any day of the week against that sneak-thief Taylor's. Fargo's bad as you are; just because he used to kind of pal around with Taylor, he don't want to think the feller's gone bad. Says we better take things easy for a bit till we find out where we're at—till we learn the truth of this business. Good Christ! What the hell's the good of them boys seein' 'em—catchin' 'em red-handed—if we're goin' to lally-daddle 'round an' wait till they gut some other ranchman? 'S what I told the Sheriff; I said, 'By God, I'm proud of you, Tanter! I'm glad to see somebody's got a little spunk yet 'round this gone-to-seed damn country.' I said I'd ride myself if it wasn't I've got the—"

"Is he goin' to try to arrest Ben Taylor?"

"He's goin' to run in every man of that crowd he can get his hands on. An' if you ask me,

Fargo's showin' mighty weak-kneed in not supportin' him. A hell of a kind of man to elect the leader of a citizens' committee! 'Wait!' he says. 'Let's not go off half-cocked, boys. We better not do nothin' brash till we learn the rights of this—'specially about Ben Taylor. Ide mightn't have seen Ben there at all—he might've been mistaken.' Hell!" Hawes swore disgustedly. "I can see Ide bein' mistaken! Ain't this whole damn country been talkin' for weeks about the way young Taylor's—"

"Yes!" cried Bella hotly. "Their tongues been wagging forty to the minute and there's not a grain of truth in anything they've said! You know how people are—Thief River people, anyway. Always looking for someone they can build up a case against; a bunch of miserable small potatoes, judging everything in the light of their own balked cravings, maligning everyone who's in any way different or decent! They're a pack of vicious curs!"

"Mmmm," he said, jaw tightening. "So that's what you think of us, is it? I guess I'm in the same corral, eh?" He looked at her oddly. "Mebbe you're right," he muttered. "Livin' in a place like this ain't much help toward turnin' out parlor dandies. But—" he said, eyes dark with a sudden anger, "by God we mind the law; an' we ain't liftin' other folks' cattle! Which is more'n you can say for your precious Ben

Taylor! That boy is crooked as a dog's hind leg. You keep away from him—hear? Not that you'll be gettin' much chance for doin' otherwise. Bett Tanter'll be takin' care of—*Here!* Where're you off to?"

"I'm goin' to bed—" she choked.

"Don't lie to me, girl!" The rocker creaked as his feet came off the table, hit the floor and surged him upright. He caught her roughly by the arm. "I know what you got in mind! You're fixin' to go hunt up that goddamn whelp an'—"

"Yes! I'm going to tell him what you said—how Ide an' the rest have framed him, and the Sheriff—"

"By God, you ain't! You're not goin' out of this house!"

Her hot, indignant eyes met his blazing ones very straightly. "I'm going to warn Ben of this trap."

He said with face held close and bitter: "If you go out of this house tonight, don't bother coming back."

Her hair shone black in the lamp's yellow glow with dancing highlights like the feathers of a grackle. It was the strength, perhaps, of this dark color gave her cheeks that so-white look. She did not flinch. She faced him calmly in the brittle quiet.

His glance shook, wavered. He seemed to be seeing something that before had escaped his notice; seemed to be realizing how bleak and drear this place could become if she went out of it. For a brief, quick-fleeting moment he appeared to be relenting. Then his cold intolerance, all the new-found harshly cruel hatred of the man who forswears friendship, got the better of him. Eyes blazing, grinding every word out like a curse, he repeated bleakly: "If you leave this house, don't bother to come back."

A kind of sigh welled from her. Then, chin up, she said:

"Goodbye."

Startled, disbelieving, he watched her wheel from the room; heard the sound of her boots going down the hall, heard them crunch the outside gravel. He smiled a little, slyly, and put his weight against the table's edge. With folded arms he waited.

Then new sound came. A saddle creaking. The smile fell off his face. He called out hoarsely: *"Wait!"*

The pound of hoofbeats mocked him.

Every instinct of her woman's nature, every tie and past relationship rebelled against thus parting with her father. Reason, logic, joined their forces, urging that she abandon this rash impulse; bidding her return before—

But reason and cold logic were not everything. There were other things as precious as the bonds of past relation; one thing certainly: loyalty. Loyalty to the man she loved.

Thoughts of her girlhood came to mind, recollections of its light and laughter, its dances gone to, its madcap pranks—all shared by Ben and Mace. But now some dark, grim thing was got afoot in this hill country, something sly, insidious and sneaking that was steadily pushing these two friends, these comrades of her youth, apart; was throwing its shadow over all this land.

The times had changed. The old life with its hayrides and its taffy-pulls was gone. Life was complex now, harsh and very real; malevolent and hateful. And, no matter how much of bitterness and anguish they might hold, its problems had to be faced.

Her determination never wavered. Ben must be warned—at once. She must reach his ranch before the sheriff, apprise him of this trap of Ide's devising and find out if he had an alibi that would stand up under Tanter's lashing. If not, then Ben must ride.

Quick pain drove its barbs through her at thought of what Thief River must be like with Ben gone out of it. But there was no alternative. If Ben was without an alibi for the time of that raid on Hockaday, he would have to go; she would *make* him go, cost what it might. Tanter and those rage-filled ranchers were no fit men to fool with. This was quick-tempered country and its denizens, once aroused, would never rest till their ideas of justice had been satisfied.

The canyon walls were spreading now, were dipping downward, leveling toward the sandy floor. The night was cold with a high wind rolling off the flanks of the Goldfield Mountains and in the heavens bright stars were glittering, filling the canyon's twistings with a murky half-light. The flogging beat of the pony's hoofs sounded very loud in the vast immensity of the night. In the wind she caught the tang of lifted dust and, startled, suddenly frantic with alarm, quirting, spurring, she drove the horse to greater speed, praying that she still might be in time.

Five minutes later, with the distant lamps of Taylor's ranch slashing yellow bars across the loamy blackness up ahead, she pulled the pony down, sent it forward at a cautious walk while her eyes stabbed the gloom of piled-up shadows.

She saw the horse abruptly. A spent animal, it was huddled on braced legs as straight as stilts. Its head hung down between the front ones, gasping muzzle scarce a hand's breadth from its quivering hocks.

She saw the figures then. The tall, frocked form of Taylor and the frailer shape against him. That would be the rider. Hurt, she guessed; Ben seemed to be supporting him—had one arm thrown across his shoulders . . .

The breath caught in her throat. Nearer now,

the true import of that still tableau smashed its brutal way across her mind. That frailer figure in Taylor's arms belonged—not to a man, but to a woman; and the startled, awkward way he whipped those arms away from her, his halting, backward step and stifled "Sho—it's Bella, ain't it?" brought Bella's world in tumbling fragments around her ears.

One longer, burdened moment she sat there in her saddle, staring, stunned, incapable of speech. With a choked cry breaking from her throat, she yanked the horse's head around and drove it, crashing headlong through the night.

Chapter Twelve
"AN' DON'T TRY ANY MONKEYSHINES!"

That night the lid came off of hell.

Within two hours of the time Fargo's meeting had been stampeded by news of Hockaday's misfortune, half Thief River was under arms and riding. Three small-spread ranches were attacked, their owners driven out and their belongings put beyond all hope of salvage. At Mesquite Flat a man whose only discovered crime was his Mormon leanings was shot and killed upon his doorstep by three masked men. A nester was killed near Castle Dome and another at Superstition. Ten miles south of Goldfield a bunch of squatter cattle were driven hellity-larrup over the lip of a hundred-foot cliff. An unidentified stranger caught drifting through the hills by scouting members of the sheriff's posse was promptly hanged from a wind-gnarled juniper and left there, dead and dangling, as a warning to his kind.

Fargo's shove for empire was under way.

Desperate, Ben had called out twice, but Bella had not waited, had not checked that passionate departure in the slightest. With the rumble of her horse's hoofs swiftly dimming in the distance he had turned to Yettem's wife, grimly bidding her get her things together and, tight-lipped, had led the dead man's bronc off in the direction of the corral.

When the woman and girl appeared upon the porch he had their rented horses ready; had a third horse saddled for himself. Picking up Jansen's body he carried it silently into the house. When he reappeared two minutes later there was a bit of folded paper in his hand. He gave it to the woman.

"I'm takin' you to Mad Spring. Kate Stalleon over there has been wantin' company ever since the last frog died in Arizona, and I reckon you'll be findin' her a right good talker—till Ace gets back," he said.

"Is there any reason why we shouldn't stay here?"

"Don't know of any," he said blandly, "except the place might get sort of lonesome. This country kind of grows on a person, but till you get to know it . . ." He looked off down the canyon, leaving the rest of it unfinished. He was lying and she knew it. From the corner of his eyes he saw her hurried glance at the darkened cabin, saw her shiver; caught the instinctive gesture with which she placed a protecting arm around the child.

He said, "If you're ready, ma'am, I expect we better be gettin' along."

It was a silent journey. Almost a flight, one might have said. Their way lay always among the thickest shadows, and when no shadows were available their horses seemed inspired to take a faster gait. They crossed a wide and shallow stream and, half an hour later, came upon another. "Fish Creek," said Taylor briefly. It was narrower than the first one, with steep and shaley banks. Its bed was cluttered with rocks and there was not much water in it. "I don't believe," Mrs. Yettem said, "we'll be able to get across here. That bank—"

"Not aimin' to," Taylor answered, and led the way upstream, in and out among the boulders, cautioning them at each bad place, yet somehow managing to make good time despite this consideration.

Presently they came to where a little way ahead another stream made juncture with Fish Creek, emptying into it from the right. "We climb out here," he said, and when they had done so he stopped them briefly for a rest.

"How much farther is it?"

"About four miles. Be there inside another hour."

They pushed on then across the moon-splashed range with the bright stars high above them and with the soughing of the wind creating haunting melody among the junipers and piñons. The woman remembered Taylor's words and looked about her curiously. It was, indeed, a wild, forbidding country; a desolate place to bring a child. And yet, the appeal was there. Bleak as was its aspect, it had grown on her already.

Forty-five minutes after putting Fish Creek behind them, they saw the lights of Kate Stalleon's roadhouse at Mad Spring.

Ben pulled the horses up. "I've got to leave you now. That's Kate's place up yonder. Just tell her you've come from me and hand her that note I gave you—"

She put a hand upon his arm, leaning forward in her saddle to peer up into his face. "Do you think"—there was a pleading in her scrutiny that made his cheeks grow darker—"do you think what happened to that man had anything to do with—to do with Ace?"

His answer came a little slower than it should have. "Shucks, ma'am," he said. "How could it?"

Her regard of him was queer. Her eyes were more than just intent; more, even, than sharply probing. The moonglow showed that plainly. There was something in them that he could not read. Her voice was soft, was husky with a hidden knowledge. "Are you sure that's all you want to say to me?"

Women were like that, he reflected; always doing and saying the unexpected. Logic—those rules by which men governed their lives—left them cold. They had their own strange code and it was something a man could never understand.

He eyed her gravely, uneasily. Was it in the cards she could have guessed—? But no; of course not. How *could* she?

As though his silence were an answer to her question, she turned away, picking up her reins and beckoning the child. They rode off and he morosely watched them; watched them till they racked their rented horses before Kate Stalleon's place. And then, disturbed, he turned his own bronc into the backtrail.

He saw it now. There'd been papers in his desk. Nothing, naturally, of an official nature, but bills, advertisements, receipts—that sort of thing. The woman would have read them, would have learned from them some portion of the truth. She would have found that he, and not Ace Yettem, was the owner of Two Bars Ranch.

Taylor rode fast, much faster than the gait by which they'd journeyed eastward—as fast as the tall blue roan could take this chancy trail. God knew if he would be in time—but he could try. Had he gone with Yettem's wife to Kate's place, his task would have been cut in half; but he had no way of knowing this and so, arrived again at Fish Creek's crossing, he swung the bronc due south on a line that would cut Thief River. He was not even thinking of the blowzy Kate. He was thinking of Bella Hawes and of the irony of fate that tonight had brought her seeking him at Two Bars—that had brought her there to find him with his arms about another woman.

Never, he thought, would he forget that look upon her face at sight of them. He did not blame her for the interpretation she had put upon the scene; the conclusion she had reached had been a natural one. Pale even yet with memory of it, square of jaw and tight of lip, he drove the roan like wildfire. He loved that tall blue horse with a passion second only to his love for Bella; but his need for speed was desperate. If he had to he would sacrifice Old Blue, for he knew that when he reached Thief River he could have his pick from Hawes' corral of the finest horseflesh in this country. And meant to—Hawes' enmity notwithstanding.

He was aware he'd no damned business going there tonight; his time was not his own and he had frittered away too much of it back there at his ranch. But he had to put things right with Bella. He believed that if he told her . . .

But the belief was lost in thoughts of the man responsible for this night's tragedies. In thoughts of the man's evil, greedy purpose, of its cause, and of the vicious means the man was using to achieve his end. Nothing—not even patriotism, could swerve Mace Fargo from his blind desire. No force—but death—could turn him from the savage swath being hacked by his ambition in its drive for a coveted crown. No force but death—and it might come to that. It might be that, in the end, Ben would have to kill him; for he had no proof—not a shred or vestige—of Fargo's connection with this thing. In his heart he knew, but such knowledge was not proof. It would have no weight were they to put the man on trial. They might smash the gang—in fact, already had affected the smoothness of its running through their vanishments of Birchman, Galloway, and Bucks Younger, through the apprehension and summary disposal of Abe Peyrolles—but they could not touch Mace Fargo. He had kept his skirts too clean and no blow leveled at the gang could reach him. Not even the squealing of some member could incriminate him, for the members they had grabbed thus far had been unable to supply convincing evidence. They'd taken a shot at that with Younger. Bucks had talked all night but couldn't clinch his argument.

Of course, they knew well enough the way things were being handled. Ben had discovered the route and the methods during those long weeks of riding that had taken him so often from Thief River. None of the parties interested had believed for a moment the fiction of his gambling; on the other hand they'd no more proof of what it was he had been up to than Ben could get of Fargo's master-minding. Trouble was, Fargo's wolves were not *demanding* proof—they were out to get Ben planted.

But Washington knew the way that Fargo's enterprise was being handled; Ben had mapped that for them to the final detail. The cattle were being lifted from Thief River ranchers, were being sent by truck to a point just short of Sawik Mountain where a German with a handy ranch was acting as receiver. From his place they were being driven in relays through the back country and on northwest across the Salt River Reservation to a new-built, cleverly hidden packing plant. Butchered, then, the beef was loaded into refrigerated trucks and hurried across California to an isolated stretch of coast that was part of the vast estate of Norman Kolbrook, the Hollywood picture king. There, in dead of night, the stolen meat was packed into motor launches that finally landed it aboard German freighters flying South American flags. The only reason Fargo hadn't brought airplanes into this business, Taylor guessed, was because of the Government's recently inaugurated investigations into the activities and cargoes of private and commercial planes being flown over coastal regions. These investigations, unfortunately, had not yet been extended to cover the perambulations of truckers. As Fargo, no doubt, had known.

It had taken real brains to figure out and fabricate a steal of this bright caliber; to figure out the necessaries required to put in motion and keep smooth-running the many varied units of so intricate a system. The thing was like a ladder; at the top was wealth, success, position, power and influence; below the bottom rung was death.

It took brains, yes; and Fargo had them. And the money Taylor's father had left in trust to put Fork Fargo's boy through college had not hurt them any. Nor had it done the world much good. That education had succeeded only in glazing a veneer of culture over Fargo's caveman instincts; it had whetted up his appetites and vouchsafed him, by comparison, a keener, more embittered perception of his own poor lot. A lot he was now in process of bettering at other people's cost.

All this Ben knew, but it was not enough. You couldn't convict a man on such stuff. In organizing the machinery of this enterprise, Mace had shown himself adroit beyond Thief River's wildest dreams. The original stealers of the beef, those men who took it off the range and loaded it into trucks, were without the faintest notion of where the steers were bound for. They did not even know the truckers who took it off their hands except as "Ed" or "Gus" or "Tony." The crew at Sawik Mountain didn't know them, either; all the German's crowd could tell you was that this variously-branded stock came in on wheels and went away by hoof. It was the same way with the outfit that took it through the mountains; with the boys who drove it into the packing plant. The butchers, though they knew the stuff was stolen, had no knowledge of its past; and once it left their hands there was nothing by which to tell it from meat slaughtered at El Paso, at Frisco, K.C. or Cincinnati. The men who took it in refrigerated trucks across the desert, across the line on into California on papers as forged and utterly worthless as the oldest rubber check, knew no more about it than did the officers of the Patrol who joked with them at the border. These men left it at Palowalla where a new set took the wheels. These drove the trucks to Beaumont where yet another crew took over and ran them down to Elsinore where Kolbrook's men took charge. These rolled them in to the great man's ocean-coast estate below San Onofre.

Of all the men who had a hand in the journey of this contraband, only Yettem, who had started it off and paid its starters from his pocket, had contact with Mace Fargo and could know of his connection; this was the hard fact Ben was up against, that had so harried his dealings with the man. Yettem was a shrewd, tough monkey, not the kind to drop any secrets—least of all to Ben; and on the other end was Kolbrook with all his money, prestige, influence.

A slick play all around and Ben admitted it. Damned near foolproof. But one of these charming nights a lot of people were going to be unpleasantly surprised. When your uncle in the striped pants steps in, money, position and influence are just so many small gods cracking; and even now the Old Boy's boot was lifting . . .

The forward-rushing rumble of loping horses cut across Ben's thinking, turning it off as a tap is turned off—instantly. His form went stiff in the saddle and a hand slid down to leather. The sound was rolling from the right, from the west, from the direction of his ranch. With quick decision he left the gun where it was and wheeled the blue roan off the trail; wheeled it into a thicket of elder where the shadows were deep and black. It took a whale of a lot of horseflesh to rack up a noise like that.

And there were a lot of horses in the group that went sawing past—ten, at least; and the moon glinted off their rifles, off the badges pinned to their vests. So at last it had come to that, Ben thought. They'd been out to Two Bars to get him.

He smiled thinly. They'd be feeling pretty boogery over a ride like that for nothing. It was just as well he had gotten himself off the trail.

He wasn't in much doubt over why they'd been to see him. Those Five Diamonds steers someone had shoved out back of the canyon were needing an explanation. That trick had been crude, very likely the work of Yettem; the man was hog-wild to get his scalp.

He listened, sitting the saddle there, until sound

of the posse's progress had grown thin and far with distance, then turned the blue back into the trail and sent it along at a canter. The posse was heading townward, there to be disbanded, Taylor guessed, for after all Bett Tanter had no business being up here; this was Maricopa County and he was sheriff of Pinal. His jurisdiction ended its northward jog at Thief River Crossing, and he knew it. Probably going down to Fargo's, Ben reflected.

He swung the roan to a faster gait. He'd better be getting this over with. Apache Junction was a long ride off and he had to send that telegram. Someone was going to catch blue hell if those Three Rings cattle weren't stopped.

Half an hour later he pulled the winded roan to a trot with the lights of Thief River's old hotel gleaming through the trees. The ford splashed beneath its hoofs and then they were stopping at the hitching rack before the hotel veranda. It was about as he'd foreseen, he thought; the posse had gone along home.

Dropping the reins, he stepped from the saddle and, with spur rowels clanking through the silence of this place, crossed the narrow porch and rapped upon the door. Rapped loudly, for he was in a hurry and it was entirely within his luck that he'd have trouble with Jesse Hawes.

He did.

Hawes came to the door himself and cursed

when he recognized Taylor. "I guess you've come to crow—"

"To crow?" Ben looked at the fellow curiously. "No, I didn't come to crow. I'd like a word with Bella, Jesse—"

"An' so would I, god damn you!" There was something unaccountably fierce and wild in the way Hawes stood and looked at him. The hate was boiling blackly in him and the fingers of one stiff-held hand were flexing. Taylor watched it fascinated. Then a thought ripped cold fear through him; and his eyes jerked up and he said quickly: "Bella's home, Jess, isn't she?"

He thought the man would choke. Hawes said: "*No* she isn't home—an' you damn well know it!" He kicked the door from his path and, cursing, lunged at Taylor, bringing a dark clenched fist past Taylor's jaw so close Ben felt the wind of it.

Jumping back Ben said: "Stop it, Jess—*stop it!* This ain't no time to go off your head. I—"

"Where is she?" Hawes growled panting. "What've you done with her, you whelp? Before God, I—"

"Take it easy, Hawes." A new voice, that; a cold voice, grim with authority. "Get them hands up, Taylor. An' don't try any monkeyshines! You know me—Bett Tanter talkin'."

Chapter Thirteen
REVELATIONS

"Yeah, I know you, Tanter," Ben said softly. "What's the big idea?"

He turned then, taking in the sheriff's pose, the oily smile, the gun held level at his hip. A portly man, Bett Tanter; a brown one with a slanted chin and eyes that said a lot of things he'd never put into words. "What's the big idea?"

"The idea is I'm placin' you under arrest. For cattle theft an'—"

"No," Ben said, shaking his head. "Not right now you're not. Put up that gun an' talk some sense. What cattle you referrin' to? That Five Diamonds stuff at my place?"

"You said it! Those steers—"

"Ain't no concern of yours," smiled Taylor.

There was a silence. Tanter breathed an oath. He said with yellow sparks in his eyes: "By God, I'll *make*—"

"Uh-uh." Taylor's head was shaking. "Come off it, Bett. Those are Five Diamonds steers all right, but they're on my spread. And my spread's clean off your reservation."

Hawes was staring from one to the other of

them darkly. "Tanter!" he shouted suddenly. "You heard what he said then, didn't you? He's *admitted* it! What the bloody hell you waitin' on? Arrest him!"

The sheriff sweated.

"Arrest him!" the old man shouted.

It was what Tanter wanted to do. It was what Mace Fargo expected of him. But there was a deterring influence in Taylor's eyes. Their sardonic amusement mocked him. They seemed to say: "Go right ahead, Tanter. Try it on if you think you're able."

Then Ben was speaking. He said through a thin grin, "Tanter, I'd take this a little slow if I were you. This ain't a good time for a man in your boots to be sticking his chin out. You can't afford to be makin' many mistakes right now, an' arrestin' me would be one. It would be a bad one. It might just be that I wouldn't surrender."

Tanter found his voice then. "Don't try to intimidate me!" he blustered. "If I saw fit to arrest you, I'd arrest you—don't think nothin' different. Happens, though, I've more important fish to fry at the moment. I have to get back to the county seat an' I ain't got no time to be botherin' 'round with prisoners. I'll give you a tip though, Taylor: if you set any store on that health of yours, you'll get clean out of this country—pronto."

Ignoring Hawes' black stare, he rammed the gun back into his holster and wheeled to get into his saddle. He was like that, hand on the horn and one foot lifted, when Taylor said: "That's white of you, Bett. I'll give you one. If you want to be real smart, cut loose of this."

The sheriff's face was livid. "I don't know what you're talkin' about! I—"

"Don't you?" Taylor said. He laughed. "I think you do. You remember Birchman, Galloway, Bucks Younger, don't you? 'Member Abe Peyrolles? Better keep those boys in mind. You'd make a poor lookin' corpse with a rope around your neck."

With a strangled cry the sheriff rammed home his spurs.

Taylor faced the startled Hawes. "So Bella hasn't come back yet, eh?"

With clamped lips Hawes stood glaring, sullen.

Taylor shrugged. "I need a couple of your horses, Jesse. I'll want the fastest ones you've—"

"You'll get no horses from me!"

Taylor regarded him bleakly. Without a word he picked up the blue roan's reins and started for Hawes' corral.

"You keep out of there!" the old man shouted.

He was shaking all over with rage. "You touch one of them broncs," he whispered, "an' I'll let you have it between the eyes!"

There was a rifle in his hands, but Taylor didn't look. Taking the rope from his saddle he shook out a loop and slipped between the bars.

• • •

Taylor was riding from town on one of Hawes' horses and leading another when a man rode out of the shadows, blocking the trail in front of him.

It was Steve Fontana.

"Nice going," he said.

Ben looked at him. "Kind of late for ridin', ain't it?"

"Just what I was thinkin'." Steve's eyes flicked over the horses. He grinned. "I heard what you told Bett Tanter. Burnin' all your bridges, eh?" He looked at Taylor curiously. "Fixin' to turn maverick?"

"Steve—" Worry rode Taylor's voice. "Bella came out to my place tonight. She—she hasn't got back. Look," he said, suddenly urgent. "You can do me a favor, Steve—Will you?"

"Sure. Want me to gun Mace Fargo?"

Taylor went taut in the saddle. There was something dark and glinting in the stare he whipped on Steve. "What made you say that?"

"You think somebody grabbed her, don't you? There ain't nobody but Fargo would pull a trick like that. *He* would."

"No," Ben said. "Mace wouldn't—"

"Well, have it that way, if you want to." Steve shrugged. "What's the favor?"

It was several moments before Ben told him. The worried look in his eyes had deepened; a touch of steel had got in them, too. He seemed to be pondering something darkly; its shadows lay on his cheeks and there was a tight look about his mouth.

His shoulders moved impatiently as though to brush the thought away. He said with a sudden gruffness: "I've got to hunt her, Steve—I've got to find her." There was a cold sweat on his face. He took something from his pocket, extended the hand toward Steve. Three folded slips of paper. Steve took them.

"Telegrams," Ben said. "Important. Will you ride to Apache Junction for me an' see that they get off?"

"Sure you don't want me to help you hunt her? That's the main thing, ain't it? Gettin' her back? These can wait—"

Ben shook his head. "They're overlate already. If you won't take them—"

"Hell," Steve said. "I'll take 'em if they're that important. Look here though, boy. Suppose you kind of take things easy till I get back. Just sort of scout around an'—"

Taylor's smile was a quick, warm thing, but didn't last. The thoughts that roved his mind left no room for it upon his face; they shoved their somber pattern across his wind-whipped moonlit cheeks and stained his tone and had their history in the curt, brief shake of his head.

"Thanks, Steve," he said. "There's no sense you gettin' mixed in this—"

"I'm in it anyway, an'—"

"No," Ben Taylor said, "I'm playin' this solo."

A restlessness stirred Fontana's shoulders. He lifted a green and slanchwise glance and stared off into the shadows. He brought the glance back to Taylor's face. He said: "You always was a goddam fool—" and then took a long breath quickly. "OK," he muttered. "Let it ride that way. I'll send your telegrams. You want I should wait for an answer?"

"There won't be any answer," Taylor said. "Get those wires off quick as you can, Steve. An' look—keep out of these hills."

"Like that, eh?" Fontana grinned.

"It's goin' to be tough," Ben said.

At Mad Spring, with the child in bed, Yettem's wife faced Kate Stalleon determinedly. "I want to know the truth. Taylor owns that ranch, doesn't he?"

Kate's tired eyes held sympathy. "Wouldn't it be better—"

"The truth!"

"Are you sure, my dear—" Kate Stalleon stopped. Her eyes were on the younger woman's face; something seen there changed her mind. She said: "It's not a pretty thing, this truth you're wanting, Madeline."

"Tell me, please. I can take it," she said doggedly. "I've been living with lies for eleven years now; the truth would be a mercy. Does Ben Taylor own that ranch?"

"Yes."

"I thought so. Yesterday I was cleaning house. In tidying up the desk I came across some papers . . . Do you know why Taylor let me go on thinking his ranch belonged to Yettem?"

"I expect he thought it was the kindest thing to do." Kate Stalleon looked down into her hands a moment. She said reflectively, "We're a hard-baked lot, us Thief River folks. We live a lot in the past 'round here, and the past, sometimes, was pretty lively. This was a gold country years ago when Father brought me into it. Thief River was a big town then, the sky was the limit and the gambling hells and honkytonks ran wide open—twenty-four hours to the day. The men were a hard, proud lot; and the women . . . well, the less said of them, the better; there were not many decent ones, three or four, perhaps—they're dead now. Ben Taylor's mother was one of them. The reason I tell you all this, I'm trying to answer your question. To understand Ben Taylor you have to understand what's back of him. In my day," she said, and sighed, "Ben's father was the Thief River marshal—Jack Taylor, the squarest, fightin'est fool in four hundred miles of territory. Ben gets a lot from him; the softness comes from his mother. It was that softness—the wish to spare you—that made him let you go on thinking

Two Bars was Yettem's ranch. Ace Yettem, to put it bluntly, is nothing but a sneaking cattle thief."

Madeline Yettem was staring into space. The expression of her still, pale face remained unaltered. She said finally, said slowly, softly, "I've thought so for a long, long while."

Kate Stalleon took a turn about the room. Her yellow hair was frowsy straw in the garish light from the chandelier. Seen beside it, the brilliant orange of her too-rouged cheeks gave her a ribald, sort of carnival look and made it doubly hard to realize there had been a day when she'd been No. 1 belle of all Thief River, the toast of a thousand throats.

She had been, though; and memory of it might have moved her now. She paused by the desk a moment, then crossing to Madeline Yettem's side she put a picture in her hands, an old-fashioned two-by-four tintype that was starting to yellow with age.

"Why, it's Ace!" exclaimed Mrs. Yettem. "Ace as a little boy. Have you noticed the resemblance to Raechel?"

"The boy in that picture was called 'Reb'—Reb Fargo," Kate said. "We had that made the day before he ran away."

"Oh; it isn't Ace?" Madeline Yettem looked up quickly. Her lips stayed parted oddly. There was a question in her eyes.

Kate said: "My married name was Fargo; that's

a picture of my boy—of one of them. I had two. This was Reb, the oldest. Ran off when he was twelve. Killed a man and had to. A bad lot; and changing his name to Ace Yettem hasn't seemed to help him much."

"Oh! Then it *was* Ace."

"Yes."

They eyed each other while the night's deep stillness thickened. Kate said abruptly: "We've that much in common, anyway. More'n a body'd think, I guess." She frowned, sat gnawing thoughtfully at a carmined lip. "I wonder . . . I wonder if he guessed that when he brought you over here—"

"You mean . . . ?"

"That Yettem's right name is Fargo—that I'm Reb Fargo's mother."

Yettem's wife stared curiously, arrested by the hunted look that flashed through the old woman's eyes. "You mean," she said, "you wonder if Taylor knew?"

Kate Stalleon nodded, though there was nothing in her face to show she'd heard. She rubbed a jeweled hand across her chin, still pondering and, inexplicably, she shivered.

Madeline Yettem said tiredly, "Does it matter?"

"Matter?" The old woman came out of her reverie to wheel a sharp, half-startled look at her. "If it didn't matter I'd not be worrying about it. Ben Taylor's nobody's fool if he *is* a chickenhearted softy. And he can be hard as the next—a damned sight harder, once he makes his mind up to it. One of these days Yettem's going too far; he'll try his luck with Taylor once too often. When that time comes, you'll be without a husband and I'll be shy a son."

Chapter Fourteen
"IT'S HAWES' KID—BELLA!"

Down in Pinal County, a good eight miles below Thief River, Mace Fargo in the Five Diamonds living room was telling Holders Hockaday: "You're not in a state of mind to think! Stick around here for a spell till you get cooled off, then maybe you can see the truth for what it is. If you can get cooled off enough—"

"I'm cool enough right now," snapped the Three Rings owner savagely. "I'm cold as a goddam icebox! But if you're expectin' me to—"

"See!" Fargo threw up his hands. "There's no use talkin' while you're in that mood. If the truth don't suit your book, you don't want any part of it—you'd rather go on thinkin' like you want to think. You're just a goddam ostrich!" He got out of his chair and crossed to a window, stood there with hands thrust deep in his pockets, letting Hockaday rave.

"If you think," growled the Three Rings owner, "I'm going to swallow that hogwash about young Taylor being with the scum that wrecked my ranch—I wouldn't take Ide's word on a stack of Gospels ten feet high!"

"You don't have to take Ide's word for anything," ground out Fargo, swinging around. "Mine's good enough for you, ain't it? The truth of the matter is, Ben Taylor was not only with them bustards like Ide says; it's *my* opinion he was *leadin'* 'em! God knows I don't want to think that any more than you do, but facts is facts, an' all your swearin'-tearin' 'round ain't goin' to change 'em."

"Leadin' 'em, eh?" Hockaday stared at him thinly. "Who put that notion in your head?"

"Look," said Fargo patiently. "As kids Ben an' me did a lot of runnin' 'round together. You know that; everybody knows it. We used to be thicker than fiddlers. Even when we was goin' to school over at Tortilla Ben had the notion when he got big he'd like to be boss of this country. Always lollin' 'round, he was, thinkin' up ways to make himself a bigshot. Used to read them paperback things about Jesse James an' the Daltons; I reckon that's what is wrong with him. You know the way Fontana moons around? Well that's the way Ben used to be; always tryin' to figure how he could grab control of the—"

"What's that got to do with Ben leadin' a bunch of cutthroat—?"

"I'm tellin' you, ain't I?" Fargo swore, exasperated. "Look: Did you ever know of rustlin' gettin' so goddam bad an' brazen as it is right now before? 'Course not; now use your head. Taylor wants to make himself—"

"Are you tryin'," demanded Hockaday, "to tell me Ben—"

"I'm tellin' you the facts!" snapped Fargo harshly. "The plain damn stinkin' facts! Taylor's slick—I give him credit; an' if you don't want to believe 'em when I'm through, that's up to you. But these are the facts an' you can't get around 'em. Somebody's makin' rustling a goddam profitable business. Ranches are being raided, burned out, gutted. Connor, Blake an' Haskelman are gone—sold their spreads an' cut for the timber. But who'd they sell to? *Nobody knows!*" He stopped and stared at Hockaday significantly. "Get it?"

Hockaday frowned. "I'll grant all that. But—"

"All right. Taylor, ever since I've known him, has wanted to boss this country. Do you know of any better or quicker way he could get control than by turnin' half the country's population against the other half? That's what he's *doing!* The little fellows against the big. The have-nots against the haves. He's got the little spreads to throw in with his bunch of rustlin' saddle tramps—an' they're set right now to clean us big fellows out of here!"

Fargo banged the desk in a way that made the pictures jump. "Once he's got us licked he'll divide this country up to suit himself. An' where will you an' me be then? Eh? Far as that goes," Fargo muttered, "where are you right now?"

Hockaday scowled. "What you've said has a sound," he admitted; "but not with Taylor back of it. Ben Taylor's—"

"Where the hell do you think he's been goin' every time he drops from sight? I'll tell you where! He's been roundin' him up this gang that—"

"If you think that, why did you try to argue Tanter out of goin' after him last night?"

"Because I was a fool, like you. Because I figured, havin' known him all my life, Ben wouldn't pull a stunt like this. But I figured wrong. Ben *did* order that raid that wrecked your ranch; he's fixin' to turn this whole damn country upside down. An' I knew it just as soon as that crowd pulled out and I'd had time to think things over. I remembered how the idea of bossin' things had been such an obsession with him in the old days. I remembered somethin' he'd said to me two-three months ago—an' it fit. It was the last little item needed to show me what he was up to, just like this wrecking of Three Rings last night was the first big step toward forcing us big ranchers into cracking down on the two-bit crowd that's backing him."

He stared at a rifle racked above the doorway somberly. "There ain't a chance I'm wrong, Holders. I only wish to God there was. But we got to face the facts."

Hockaday said: "I can't get pat with your

reasoning. In the first place, I don't believe Taylor's the fellow back of this. And if he is, why in hell would he be *wantin'* the big outfits to go gangin' up on his crowd?—if it's true the little fellows *have* thrown in with him, which I doubt." He looked at Fargo skeptically. "Got the answer to that tucked up your sleeve?"

"I haven't got anything up my sleeve," said Fargo wearily.

"Kick in, then. What's the answer?"

"The more I talk to you, Holders, the more I think the fellow that said about there bein' no fool like an old fool must've run across you someplace in his travels."

Hockaday's cheeks got a little red. "Never mind that," he said. "Tell me why Taylor would be wantin' the big outfits to go crackin' down on the fellows that's joined up with him—"

"That's why," Fargo told him. "To be sure they *stay* joined up with him. Which they'll have to in sheer self-defense if he prods us into jumpin' them—"

"But you been *advocatin'* jumping them," growled Hockaday. "What the hell was—"

"Sure. But that was before I got wise to Taylor being back of this."

"By Heaven!" breathed Hockaday. "Have you got *all* the answers?" And then he said: "It seems to me that for a guy who knows so goddam much, you been doin' a powerful lot of blunderin'!"

"I have been. I admit it," Fargo muttered. "It's what comes of refusin' to see the truth about a thing just because the fellow it concerns used to do his wenching with you. It's this mistaken idea of friendship that's been givin' the guy his chance. But it's all over far as I'm concerned. I got my eyes open now an' I'm goin' after him—friend or no friend."

The way that Hockaday rasped a hand across the ends of his mustache hinted of a mind far less assured than that mind had been. He got out a pipe and grimly packed its bowl with smoking. Cold, sardonic amusement was agleam in Fargo's eyes, but Hockaday did not see this because Fargo had gone again to the window and stood with his back turned, looking out.

In the act of scratching a light, the Three Rings boss remembered something. "You was mentioning something Taylor said—the thing that made you realize he was back of this. What was it?"

"He said," declared Fargo, " 'If I ever see the chance, I'm goin' to grab me off this country. There's a fortune here in cattle if a guy could get rid of the deadwood. Be a lot of toes stepped on, I reckon. But if I get my mind set to do it, boy, don't ever get in my way, because once I start there'll be no stopping me—remember that. No friend is worth one-quarter what this country's worth to me.' "

"He said that?" cried Hockaday, startled.

"Would I be sayin' so if he hadn't? I got my schoolin' on Taylor money, Holders. I owe the name aplenty—*plenty*. But not so goddam much—" he checked himself. He said with sudden anger: "Did you know he offered to buy me out? Well, he did. Over at Tortilla the other night before he tangled with Yettem. Offered me a hundred thousand, cash, to turn Five Diamonds over an' clear out."

His cheeks were purple and his voice shook so with feeling, he had to stop a little to get hold of himself. When he spoke again his words were gruff—were curt with the effort he put forth to control his temper. "It wasn't Five Diamonds he wanted. He was scared to have me 'round here account of what he'd told me. He was afraid I'd guess his game and mebbe spill the works and stop him."

It was difficult to correctly gauge the emotion in Hockaday's eyes. But he was not indifferent to Fargo's talk. He frowned through the haze of pipe smoke and stared absorbedly into space. He was about to speak when hoof sound drove its warning across the yard. Fargo, whirling from the window, doused the lamp and from the region of the bunkhouse taut voices snapped their challenge.

"Bett Tanter," came the call.

Fargo relit the lamp and the sheriff joined them,

bringing the chill of the moonlit trails in with him and, puffing, dropped heavily into a chair as though it had been himself and not the horse had made that run.

Fargo said: "What's up?"

"The devil, by the look!" Tanter's grin was ghastly. "The fool's got started, Mace—hell's poppin' clear to Castle Dome." He scrubbed a hand across his chin. "Last night we chased a circle clear 'round Fish Creek Mountain without catchin' so much as a cold. This mornin', early, couple of the damn fools in my posse grabbed some saddle tramp and swung him for the hell of it. It's gettin' so you can't even trust your own friends any more. I remembered Ide's tale tonight and swung a loop past Two Bars, but the place was empty—Taylor's gone. I disbanded the boys when we got to town, an' then, right after they'd cleared out, the news started comin' in—"

"What news?"

Tanter looked at Fargo sullenly. "You hadn't ought to 'a' crossed me up like that, Mace. You said you'd keep your crowd in hand—"

"My crowd—if you mean the hands I got on my payroll—ain't left this place since you pulled out of here last night."

"They ain't?" said Tanter blankly. He dragged a bandana from his pocket then and mopped his gleaming face. "Good Christ! That means Taylor ain't waitin' for no excuse then; he's makin' him one to order. Three one-horse spreads belongin' to his friends went up in smoke last night. A nester got killed at Superstition—another one near Goldfield. That Mormon guy at Mesquite Flat was riddled on his doorstep, an' the hills is full of ridin' fools with rifles across their saddles. I was fired at four times comin' down here! It's God's own mercy I got here at all!" He sat there puffing, fanning his face with his hat and looking everywhere save at Hockaday.

Not that Hockaday was eying him. The Three Rings boss was thinking of Fargo's words, and the scowl that rode his cheeks got steadily darker and darker.

Fargo was watching him closely, and when Hockaday looked up he said to Tanter: "That ain't all. There's somethin' else botherin' you. Spill it."

The sheriff stammered. He scrubbed a hand around the inside of his collar. "It's Hawes' kid," he blurted. "Bella—she's been kidnapped! Taylor's taken her into the hills!"

They sat there, frozen. Then, "Merciful Christ!" cried Hockaday, and came surging to his feet with cheeks gone black as hate. "Come on," snarled Fargo, sprinting for the door. "I'll hunt him down an' kill him if it's the last damn thing I do!"

"Wait!" yelled Tanter desperately. "The Committee—"

"Go get 'em if you want 'em! I ain't waitin' on nothin'!"

• • •

Inside short minutes, Five Diamonds was in the saddle and tearing northward. The trail was black, but not a tenth so black as the soul of the man who led them. Deep within him Fargo laughed—an obscene jeer, a gloating.

Chapter Fifteen
CAMP THREE

Taylor lay with his head turned upslope, striving to penetrate the sultry twilight of the trees. This was thirty miles north of Gonzales Wells, Camp Three on the cattle trail, last stop this side of the California Line. Hawes' horses were showing thin, gaunt with the strain of the grueling demands he'd made upon them. If she wasn't here—

Cautious always, as his marshal father had taken time to teach him to be almost soon as he could sit a saddle, Taylor's stare raked the rim of that aspen-studded hollow with a patient care. His cheeks were thinned, beard-stubbled and thick with the dust of the long hard miles behind him. His shirt, like the rest of him, was grayed with trail grime and his gambler's pants had lost their crease. There were chaparral scratches across his coat. The glass bottle shine was gone from his boots. Here was a man who'd come down in the world; he had the look of a fugitive and his habits were in keeping. And he *was* a fugitive, if it came to that. He wasn't kidding himself. Fargo, now that the ball was rolling, would be out to get him any way he could.

And the ball was rolling. Make no doubt of that. Drifting punchers, line riders, saddle tramps—even the few responsible cowmen he bumped into, all were talking of it. The word was on everybody's tongue. "Keep away from Thief River, boy—there's a war goin' on down there." From the Salt clear on down through the Superstitions, men were dying with their boots on, and folks who had any business down in that country were postponing it. Reports conflicted, told incidents varied and details were meager. Descriptions vague beyond recognition were eagerly appended to each recounting of the fracas. But one thing all were sure of: momentous events were brewing and the Thief River region was locked in a bloody struggle none could see the end of.

In the five days since he'd left it, Taylor heard, eight more spreads had gone up in smoke. Isolated two- and three-man outfits mostly, but at least one other big ranch had been ravaged and left gutted: Ham Meeker's Whip over in the footslopes of the Goldfields. The little outfits, rumor said, had joined up with the rustlers and were doing their almighty damnedest to put the big brands out of business. No one knew what had started the trouble; some said this and some said that; one crazy story had it that a guy named Taylor had run off with another fellow's girl; another popular version was that a Ben somebody-or-other had organized the riffraff and was out to take the country over. But all agreed that Thief River was a damned good place to stay away from.

In five days' riding, Ben had covered a lot of territory, but he had not found the girl. He had not even word of her. Guessing at the start that Mace was much too slick to chance having Bella discovered on his ranch, Ben had not gone near Five Diamonds. Entrusting the dispatching of his delayed reports to Steve, he had built a dust northwestward on the trail of the stolen cattle, thus linking desire with duty; but it had not gotten him much. Somewhere along this trail, he'd believed, they'd be holding the girl a prisoner, but he had not come up with her yet.

He had been to Sawik Mountain. For hours he had scouted the German's ranch in vain and finally, convinced they were not holding her there, had pushed into Indian country. But she hadn't been in the badlands, either; the relay camps strung out across them seemed without any knowledge of her. She'd not been hidden at Camp Two; long had he watched those shacks about the packing plant, only in the end to be convinced they'd taken her farther. Tight of mouth and bleak of eye, he'd struck straight west for this secret layout north of Gonzales Wells. She might not be here, either, but it were better not to think of that.

His shoulders moved impatiently. He couldn't hunt for her much longer; too much time had been squandered now—time that didn't belong to him. Yet deep inside he knew he'd never quit until he found her—not even if they swung him for it. Let them call it treason, they could call it what they wanted, but Bella Hawes meant more to him than forty thousand cattle!

He knew what they would say, all right. That range war raged in the mountains, that a county was going bankrupt and that men were dying because he'd found no way to stop Mace Fargo from this mad, vicious drive for empire. Well, let them say it! What had they expected of him? That he strangle Fargo with his own two hands? Perhaps he should have; after all, what was one man's life when balanced against the things at stake? The fate of hundreds—perhaps of millions, might well hinge on the outcome of this thing, for Fargo, when you came right down to it, was trifling with the nation's safety. He—

Ben pulled his head up, listening. For some time he'd been aware of the throbbing hum of distant motors. Steadily that hum had grown in volume. Now he caught the screech of brakes, the halloo of greetings, a sudden stillness as the unseen drivers cut their motors off. More refrigerated beef, was Taylor's thought. And then voice sound, jumbled and excited, drifted down to him on the wind; and there was a stirring up of shadows off yonder among the trees.

He wriggled backward, got his horse. It was now or never. He risked a quick look at his gun, eased it back to leather and swung grimly into the saddle. He could not wait longer. She was here; she had to be. And if there were many things he did not know, many questions to which he had no answers, one thing experience had taught him well. That a bold hand was the best defense that any man could have.

So he'd play it bold.

Leading his spare mount, he rode in among the trees. There were three big vans there, parked without lights before a long and barracks-like cabin. A dark grouping of figures showed near one of them, and for a moment the voices of these men covered Taylor's approach. Then a man came out of the cabin, saw him, started to join the others, then looked again more carefully. "What—" He broke off sharply, dropping his left hand beltward.

"Who's bossin' this?" Ben hailed him.

"Who the hell are *you,* an'—"

"I asked," growled Taylor, "who's in charge," and saw the others turning then with raking, distrustful stares. A man wheeled backward into the cab and a truck's lights bit an instant lane through the cluttered gloom, throwing the cabin front into a kind of stage-set-like relief, blotting all else into inky blackness.

Caught in that glare Taylor did not move. It was a test to sorely try the strongest nerves. He did not bat an eyelash. One false move—the least sign of hesitation now, would sign his death warrant. "I haven't all night," he said harshly. "Who's bossin' this? Speak up!"

The fellow in the doorway, the man who'd started to go for his gun, eased the hand away a little from the .45 that was slung butt-forward against his right hip. He exchanged a worried glance with one of the truckers. Ben could guess their thoughts; this would have been ludicrous if it had not been so serious. The man in the doorway, still hesitant, licked his lips. "Look," he said, "I don't know you from Adam—"

"Talk, damn you! Talk an' talk fast!"

With gone-white cheeks the man said hurriedly: "Stoil—Gleed Stoil."

"Stoil!" Taylor cried. "Damn you, don't lie to me! Stoil belongs at Camp Four!"

"He's been transferred—sent over here account of Tyrone bein' took with the chickenpox—"

"Where's Stoil now?" Taylor's voice was curt.

"He's—" the man wouldn't meet his eyes. "He's down to the Wells—"

"Why? Why isn't he here where—"

"He oughta be gettin' back here pretty quick—" began some Good Samaritan, and suddenly lost all interest in the alibi. He cringed, backed away a step before the look in Taylor's eyes.

Ben ignored him. Getting out of the saddle, he started for the doorway, walking softly on the balls of his feet. The eyes of the fellow standing there showed big and scared. But he held his place, a hand gripped rigidly to the frame at either side. "Whoa up! You don't come a step inside till Stoil gits here—"

"I don't *what?*"

The man's cheeks were gray and pulpy, but he did not budge. Scared he plainly was; but he was game, too. He said thickly, said desperately dogged: "Nobody gits inside till Stoil gives the word. Them's my orders an'—"

"I see," interrupted Taylor, and his voice was silky smooth. "I'll have to give you new ones. *Get away from that door before I salivate you.*"

It looked like it would come to that. A clock's sound beat the silence with increasing loudness. Ben, still walking forward, was close enough to see the conflict of fear with duty in the fellow's dilated eyes before, with a sudden strangled cry, the man convulsively jerked aside.

Fear had triumphed, but it was a hollow victory to Ben. With the vacated doorway still two feet beyond, a motor's hum came purring across this sticky hush to stop him, to lock him in his tracks with the bitterness of despair.

He could not risk it now. A moment more and he'd have been inside; would have known for sure whether Bella was being held here.

But he dared not enter now with that motor's sound throbbing nearer, nearer . . . That would be Stoil returning from the Wells and, knowing Stoil's uncertain temper, knowing the violent, unpredictable nature of the man, he dared not chance the possibilities in case the girl were in there. Better to be trapped here in this damned truck's glare than to risk the chance of Bella's stopping lead meant for himself.

But the hand was dealt now. He had to play it, come what might. At least he could be glad of one thing—that Stoil and he had met before and that Stoil, tough, unpredictable and rancorous as he knew the man to be, had accepted him for the long rider he'd pretended being while doing that work which finally had resulted in uncovering Fargo's perfidy.

Everything depended now on Stoil; on the sort of humor the man was in and on Stoil's continued acceptance of him as one of their own kind. If things worked right he might play out this bluff and make it stick. But if Stoil had found him out—

He eased himself around a bit, braced one shoulder against the wall. Thus placed, jaw clenched in an impatience not altogether pretended, he waited out Stoil's coming.

Chapter Sixteen
WAY OF THE TRANSGRESSOR

"Well?" Mace Fargo's glare was ominous. "I'm still waitin'. Cat got hold of your tongues? I want to know why Thurman's place wasn't wrecked last night accordin' to the plan. I want the reason—an' by God," he whispered huskily, "it better be a good one!"

Monk Ide stared at his untouched glass of whisky, exchanged a worried glance with Yettem. "Tell him," Yettem said.

Ide's dark and hammered face slewed around and his cold-jawed mouth twitched sideward in a sneer. But when he came to speak, his knowledge of the language, under Fargo's grim regard, seemed suddenly to desert him. He shifted his feet uneasily and licked his lips till Fargo in a fury surged from his chair to tower above him. "Will you talk," Fargo gritted wickedly, "or shall I choke the damn truth out of you?"

Two days had passed since the coming of the sheriff that night with his lies for Hockaday's hearing. Two days that had held other drawbacks than their failure to find Ben Taylor. Thief River wasn't reacting quite as Fargo had planned to the stimulus being fed it. For one thing, this war was not progressing as swiftly as he'd hoped for; and the little guys—those two-bit outfits clinging by their teeth to the skirts of the big spreads' ranges—were showing an unexpected stubbornness in their dogged refusal to lend his program the aid expected of them. Already six small spreads had seen their hopes and homes and everything else they had, fed to the flames that turned the night skies bright—flames fanned by Yettem's raiders, and plenty others had gotten a taste of the steel in watching their cattle and broncs run off—in seeing the rest of their four-footed profits hamstrung right under their eyes. But they'd made no attempt to form into gangs; to carry this war to the big spreads' doorsteps. A bunch of yellow curs. Bewildered, baffled, beaten and licked without ever turning a hand. It was enough to make a fellow retch! Cursing their spineless submission, Fargo had ordered Ham Meeker's place razed and, to speed things up, had passed the word that Thurman's place be put to the torch at the same time. Meeker's Whip was a thing of memory in ashes, but Thurman was conducting his business as usual—leastways he still was able.

Snapping forward, Fargo caught Ide's shoulder in a grip that made him wince. "What happened?"

A sulky brilliance got into Ide's eyes. He looked at Yettem across Mace's shoulder and spat grimly into the fireplace. "I guess," he said, "we was scared."

"Scared?" Fargo's ruddy face veered around to slash a look at Yettem. "God damn it, I told you Saturday, Ace, you'd ought to use more men—"

"That wasn't it," Ide said, and Fargo, turning, found his look at once considering and speculative. Ide's eyes were queer as he repeated slowly: "That wasn't it."

"Then what was it?" Fargo demanded.

Ide countered with a question. "How much did it cost you to buy up Tanter?"

Fargo stared. For a second it looked like temper would have its way with him. Then he said thinly, said very softly: "Five thousand, cash, an' my influence next election."

Monk Ide nodded meaningfully. "That's your answer."

"You talk like a fool. What do you—"

"Look," drawled Ide, shaking loose of his arm. "You pay Bett Tanter five grand to keep out of this or trail his luck with yours. Tanter's star takes care of Pinal County, but most of this ruction's takin' place up north—up in Maricopa. Chris Tingley figures to be a heap more wolf than Tanter ever dreamed of bein'. You didn't offer him—"

"I didn't offer him nothing," Fargo grunted. "His head's too—"

"Then you better start offerin' pronto if you want we should keep on with this . . ." He stopped, sardonically eyeing Fargo who had whirled impatiently on Yettem and was demanding: "What is the damn fool talking about? If you know, for Christ's sake put it in plain language an'—"

Yettem snarled: "The reason we didn't wreck Thurman's place was because Chris Tingley with a hell's own smear of deputies was camped down all around it with a bunch of .45-90's, jest waitin' fer us to show!"

That rocked the Five Diamonds boss clear back to the edge of his bootheels. It was like a slaughter-house maul had smashed him across the shoulders. All the lines of his face broke up and his eyes showed stunned, incredulous. Then a black, soul-shaking anger jumped its sudden flame across them and a raging fury made a whistling sound of the breath sucked through his teeth and he started cursing, loosing his flaying epithets on Yettem and Ide impartially, and was reaching for another breath when Ide started for the door.

Fargo's grip, like a striking snake, snapped out and spun him around. Fargo's face was bloated, poisonous. He slammed Ide's back against the wall and was doubling up his fist when Ide, white and shaken and pinned there as he was, choked huskily: "Get your goddam hands off me—get 'em off, I say!" And Fargo, wild eyes raking downward, saw the cold thing gleaming at Ide's waist.

He backed off, teeth bared and muscles jerking.

"Don't take your grudges out on *me*," Ide whispered smokily. "I ain't your dog an' I don't have to take that stuff. I work for you when it suits my book an' not one damn bit longer!"

Fargo, silent, made a stiff and sultry shape against the light-glare from the window. They watched him scrub a hand across his eyes and shake himself. He was like a man coming out of a stupor. He looked at Ide then with a smoldering, grudging interest. "Forget it," he said thickly, and wheeled across to the table and poured himself a stiff one from the opened bottle there.

But Ide kept his gun in hand with narrowed, watching eyes distrustful. And Yettem, still rigid, held his sunburned cheeks strictly neutral.

They were like this when across the waiting stillness came the muted sound of hoofbeats. Not a hurried pound, that sound, but one drawing steadily nearer. They kept their places, listening, till it hit the yard outside. A man's fist drummed loud echoes from the cedar door. Gruffly Fargo called: "Come in."

It was the Pinal sheriff, Bett Tanter.

He gave them a nervous, catlike glance and lumbered across the room and dropped his bulk in the Morris rocker like a too-full sack of meal.

"What do you want here?" growled Fargo, irritated.

"That's a nice fine way for a man to talk to the guy that's keepin' him afloat—"

"Get on with it," Fargo muttered. "We're busy here—havin' a meetin'."

Tanter looked at them. Fargo said with his voice turned ugly: "Well?"

The sheriff sweated. "You—" He said: "You ain't goin' to like this very good." He hesitated, nervously mopping at his face with a grimy handkerchief already wet. "Mace," he said at last, "these one-hoss spreads has got the law on you—they've swored them out a warrant an' I been ordered to arrest you . . ."

"Are you crazy?" demanded Fargo. His ruddy face flushed darkly. He caught Tanter by the shoulder, jerked him upright out of his chair. "Say that again!"

"It's God's truth, Mace." He swerved scared eyes from Fargo's stare. "They come into my office not four hours ago. They had Judge Blackton with 'em an' a warrant—claimed you was tryin' to run 'em out of the country! I told 'em—"

"Where is this warrant?"

"Right here." Tanter dug it from a pocket, passed it over. "Blackton said—*Hey!* You can't—"

"The hell I can't," Mace said, and threw the tatters of the warrant in Tanter's face. "There's your warrant. Go ahead an' serve it."

Putty-cheeked and quivering, Tanter eyed the fluttering fragments. His look was the look of a man who has seen his gods kicked bodily from the temple and awaits in shuddering expectancy the thunder that will herald grim retribution.

But nothing happened.

Fargo grinned at him like a wolf. "I'm the law," he jeered. "Wake up! I'll have Blackton off that bench before the sun goes down. Get back to your hole an' get those papers fixed on Grierson. We're closing him out."

Tanter stared aghast. "On *Grierson* . . . Man, I can't do that!" he cried. "Do you realize what you're askin'? Why, it—it ain't *legal!*"

"You better make it legal. I want him out by three o'clock."

The sheriff choked. "Do you want to see me *killed?*"

"I can get along without you. By three o'clock, remember. If at three you're not in possession of Grierson's ranch, there'll be a new sheriff appointed for this county. His first act," said Fargo coldly, "will be to issue 'dead-or-alives' for the apprehension of ex-Sheriff Tanter—'wanted for the cold-blooded hanging of an unidentified stranger.'"

Cheeks gray as dried rock-moss, Tanter stumbled through the door.

"Expect I'd better amble myself," Ide murmured. He'd put his pistol up at the sheriff's coming, but had a hand still casually draped across its butt.

Fargo, watching that hand, said: "No hard feelings?"

"No hard feelings."

"Good!" Fargo said. "I want—"

"Mebbe you better pull that raid yourself," Ide drawled.

"You throwin' me over?"

"Let's say I've read the writin' on the wall." A cramping strain licked through the flatness of Ide's watching eyes. "I got a sick aunt or a uncle, or mebbe I got to bury my gran'mother or something. Anyhow—"

"God damn you!" Fargo shouted. "You fixin' to rat on me?"

Ide said very gently: "You're a little fast for me, friend Mace. I'm jest a two-bit rustler that likes to take things leisure-like. I like the sun an' the stars an' the sound of the wind in the trees—"

"You can't quit me now!" Mace snarled.

"That may be so," Ide said, "but I can damn well try."

And, smiling briefly, bleakly, he backed himself through the door.

Yettem looked at Fargo curiously.

"The bustard!" Fargo's cheeks were black with fury. "Tell the boys to stop him—to *stop* him! Do you understand? That fool's going straight to Taylor!"

"Uh-uh." Yettem shook his head. "He won't

be tellin' Taylor anything. We don't know where Taylor's at—"

"Never mind! Tell the boys to stop him! When a guy signs on with me, he stays signed on—*or else!* He's to be drilled on sight. You pass the word around. Now look—" Fargo eyed him grimly. "I want Thurman put out of business; I want it tended to tonight. You're to see to it and I don't want any more slip-ups. They're holdin' his beef herd up at Clover Canyon; load it into trucks an' get it started for the coast—"

"Not me," Yettem said emphatically. "Not me, boy—not with Sheriff Chris Tingley—"

"Tingley's at Thurman's ranch, you fool. You told me that—"

"Mebbe so. But Thurman's whole damn crew's holdin' down that beef cut—"

"What of it? You got plenty men. Get more if they ain't enough. What the hell's come over you?"

Yettem licked his lips. He said: "The Government—"

"To hell with the goddamn Government!" shouted Fargo. "What in God's name is it but a bunch of damn stuffed shirts? Fellas like you an' me; only they happened to get the breaks, so now they crack the whip for the rest of us—money talks with them just like it does with Tanter. An' once we're fixed—Hell! We'll be able to bargain with the best of 'em. What you worried about?

They got to have proof, ain't they? They can't pin a thing on us—"

"Not on you, mebbe," muttered Yettem sullenly.

"Nor on you, either! I'm backin' you, ain't I?"

Yettem was thinking that Fargo once had given that promise to Ide and Tanter, too; but he had better sense than to mention it. "Somethin'," he said, "might slip—"

"Don't be a fool!" said Fargo gruffly. "Nothing's going to slip—an' if it does, they won't snare *us* in it. Look: Kolbrook's taking the money; Kolbrook will take the rap. If he wriggles clear, there's plenty guys between us an' him. Besides, by the time the Government gets any proof, we'll *own* this goddam country! Nobody'll put any skids under *us*.

"Now look, you can crack old Thurman easy as guttin' a slut. There's plenty of guys for the hirin'. You get yourself a bigger bunch an' ram down on that beef. Let a couple of Thurman's crew get clear to carry word; while they're rushin' it to Thurman you can get your vans piled full an' on their way. Then you cut a circle. Hit Thurman's buildings from the south. Tingley an' all his deputies'll be ridin' hell-for-leather on the trail of that rustled beef—I doubt if there'll be three men at the ranch. Why, the thing's a cinch! You won't be taking any chance at all!"

Yettem's look held no conviction. Sweat made a shine across his forehead and the hands that gripped his chair arms showed a nervousness he could not hide. He jammed them in his pockets and got up. He said, cheeks scowled with worry: "I don't like it. I don't like any part of it. And that kidnappin'—"

"We've hung that onto Taylor—"

"Makes no difference. If we ever get tripped up . . . This thing's too goddam big!" he snarled. "You're gettin' beyond your depth! 'F I'd known you meant to go so far—"

"You wouldn't have got mixed up in it," sneered Fargo.

"You're damn well shoutin' I wouldn't! Why, the things you've pulled—" Yettem stopped. He dragged a long breath through clenched teeth. "You've had the devil's own luck. But you'll take that bucket to water once too often. If I had my way—"

"We're having *my* way for a change." Fargo struck a softer note, made his boast with a sureness that had fooled wiser men than Yettem. "Another three nights," he said, "—say four nights at the most, an' we'll have the whole thing licked. There won't be enough opposition left to stick in a lady's teacup. We'll own this country from the Superstitions clear beyond the Salt—an empire! God, Ace, think of it! Fork Fargo's boys, lords of all Thief River!"

"Ahr—you sound like a goddam Alger!" Dark, scowling, Yettem strode about the room as though some premonition rode him. Furtively, from time to time, his distrustful eyes shot squinted looks at Fargo, black as holes burned in a blanket. Then suddenly he came out with it. "You're forgettin' that damn Ben Taylor!"

"Hell, he won't dare show his face 'round here—"

"If he's a Gov—"

"Bah! If he was a Government dick we'd never have got that last beef through—"

"You don't know if we *did!* Don't none of us know, nor *won't* till the first of the month. You take a hell of a lot too much for granted! Dammit, I've told you forty times—"

"I know. You got Taylor on the brain," Mace jeered. "I tell you the man's washed up!"

Goaded, Yettem snarled: "That's what the ol' man said about your fa—" and stopped with his mouth still open, twisted. Panic stared from his eyes and his shoulders dug the wall as Fargo came for him, dark with fury.

"God damn you!" Fargo cried. "I've had enough of your stinkin' hints an' innuendos!" His hands got Yettem's throat and Yettem's head slammed into the wall and Fargo shook him till his eyes looked like they'd burst. Then Fargo stood back and sank his right to the wrist in Yettem's midriff and, as the lanky raider doubled, straightened him with a smoky hook to the chin. This was not the first time Yettem had made some veiled or enigmatic, some derogatory allusion to the big man's parentage; but Fargo intended it to be the last. In the grip of that towering rage, it was God's own mercy he didn't kill the fellow. As it was, Yettem couldn't stand when Mace let go of him; he stumbled, went lurching sideways and crashed against the table, carrying it with him to the floor and lying there half-conscious, gasping, groaning, tangled in its wreckage.

Mace stood over him, big fists clenched, still shaking with his passion. He bent abruptly, got a grip in Yettem's shirt, and hauled him bodily to his feet. "Start talkin', you snake! I want the truth an' I'm goin' to get it if I have to beat you into a pulp!"

Yettem's head lolled. His eyes were glazed and black and blue and all that kept him on his feet was Fargo's grip. Fargo shoved him against the wall.

"Talk an' talk quick!"

Yettem bleared at him stupidly. He was still punch drunk, incapable of grasping either threats or questions.

Fargo slapped him across the face. "Who *was* my father?"

Yettem groaned. He lifted still-dazed bloodshot eyes, cringing away from Fargo's scowl.

Fargo's voice bit at him. "Answer, damn you!"

Wobbly, Yettem swayed in Fargo's grip.

Fargo, savage and impatient, shook him;

slapped him again across the face—hard this time, hard enough that every finger mark showed livid on Yettem's skin. "Who was he?"

"Taylor—Square Jack Taylor," Yettem whispered.

"That's a lie! A dirty goddam lie!"

The raider tried to duck, but his nerves were not quite up to it. Fargo's fist, blood-spattered, struck his face with a meaty impact and he went down the wall like an empty sack. He lay where he stopped, grotesquely sprawled, unmoving.

Fargo had a boot drawn back to kick him when a voice said gruffly back of him: "For shame, Mace Fargo! Do you want to kill your brother?"

Fargo spun in his tracks, lips writhing.

Kate Stalleon stood in the doorway.

Chapter Seventeen
THREAT AND PROMISE

Taylor watched Stoil climb from the car. It was like something from a play, the way the man stood paused a moment staring across that glare—like Washington about to cross the Delaware—like Paul Revere paused to catch the sound of British rowlocks. For that fraction of time Stoil was utterly still, then his breathing deepened and he grunted something and came tramping across the truck-lit yard with head held high like a hound with its nose to the wind.

He was squat and pot-bellied, a man with a granite face. A man, Taylor knew, who had gotten his wants by ramming his way down other folks' throats. A lot like Fargo in some respects—he could be as bull-headed and ruthless. But he hadn't the younger man's vision; was more given to violence and much less to the use of his brains. His cud of tobacco bulged a beard-stubbled cheek and his hair, iron-gray, made a careless tangle across a forehead of pressed-up wrinkles. His greasy cotton shirt flapped open from collar to waistband. A valued publicity, disclosing the hair-matted chest of a gorilla. He had the gorilla's sad, sleepy-lidded eyes, and a gorilla's soul behind them, as a number of men could have told you had they been above the grass-roots.

He had been a sheepman once and still smelled strongly of them as he stopped in front of Taylor. "Howdy, Braley," he said gruffly. "What brings you 'round here again?"

Taylor said: "We better talk more private." Stoil stared a moment longer, then turned his regard on the others. He had a nod for the man in the door who stepped immediately away from there and vanished beyond the radiance. "Cut those lights," he said, and the yard went instantly dark. "Come along," he said to Ben, and led the way inside.

The shades were drawn. A lamp, turned low, burned on the desk. Stoil shoved a chair at Ben and dropped down on the sofa. "What's on your mind? Come over about this beef?"

"No; but keep it here. Don't send any more on until you're told to." There was no expression on Ben's lean face. "I'm here about the girl."

"Girl?" There was no expression on Stoil's face either. "What girl?"

Ben looked at him intently. "Let's cut the horseplay," he said softly. "I've come for that girl Yettem sent you."

Stoil rasped a hand across his chin, took the hand away and looked at it. "Somebody's been loadin' you, Braley. No girl's been sent to me."

"Maybe they called her a boy," Ben said; "a sick man—some fellow shot up in a raid. The point is, Yettem sent somebody over here and I've come after 'em."

Gleed Stoil said nothing—not even a "Did he?" or "Have you?" He just lolled there on the sofa, a tough, squat lump of a man with a granite face that locked away his thoughts.

"Now, look," Ben said. "I haven't got all night, Gleed. I got a long ride ahead of me before morning. Maybe you been expecting a written order or something. Well, I haven't got one. They told me to ride on over here an' get the girl and— Oh, yes; I was to tell you it would be all right. They're shiftin' her to another hideout."

And still Gleed Stoil said nothing. He kept on sitting and he kept on looking, but he didn't open his mouth.

It was enough to get on anyone's nerves, and Ben's were not at their best. Edgy, he leaned forward, grimly tapped Stoil on the knee. "If this is your notion of humor, Stoil, you better get shucked of it pronto. I've come here after that girl and I ain't figuring to leave without her."

Then Stoil spoke. "Mebbe," he said, "you ain't goin' to leave."

Ben Taylor sat very still. "Ain't goin' to, eh? Why not?"

"I ain't give the matter much thought yet. But I been hearin' about you, boy. They claim you're a holy terror with a gun—That right?"

Ben mentally shook himself. It seemed this

fellow was deeper than a man would guess. If he'd found out the truth of Ben's relations with the gang, why didn't he out with it? Why wasn't he holding onto a pistol, doing his talking over its muzzle? Puzzled, uncertain, but still in full control of himself and determined to make a fight of it if Stoil should reach for his belly-gun, he said:

"Expect I could make out to use one. But look, I'm in a hurry. Suppose you fetch the girl an' let me ride."

But Stoil sat doggedly on, his gray eyes never blinking. Ben had no way of gauging what was going on in his mind. Maybe nothing was. But it looked pretty much like he was onto Ben's imposture. And it was pretty certain too that when he got around to it he was going to do something about it.

It looked like he was trying to wear Ben down, to garner that much advantage toward the time when he made his break.

Ben cocked his muscles and waited. He waited till it became a physical impossibility to hold himself still any longer. He was just fixing to drag his gun and pray for luck when Stoil said abruptly:

"How they treatin' you over there?"

Ben let his breath out softly. "I'm doin' all right."

"Gettin' a big cut out of these tinhorns?"

"So-so."

"Just as lief get more, I guess?"

"I could use more." Ben stared thoughtfully around the room. Bella was not in here. If she were at this camp they were holding her someplace else. Some shed, some barn or outhouse. He brought his glance back to Stoil. "You got some friend in mind who's needin' a hired-gun hombre?"

It was then that Stoil really startled him. "I could use a guy like you myself," he said. "How about it?"

Was the fellow playing with him? Or was he really, seriously in earnest? "I'd have to hear the proposition," Ben said carefully.

Stoil eyed him a moment longer. Then, leaning forward, he sketched his plan. It was briefly put and beautifully simple. There was a ton of money, he said, in this new racket of Yettem's. But why let Yettem lick the gravy? Why not muscle in on some themselves? The cash, he said, was handed over on the coast—Oh, yes; the cattle went that far—and mailed to Camp Four in a package labeled "Branding Fluid"— that newfangled chemical crap being sponsored by some old woman's cruelty-to-dumb-animals outfit. At Camp Four the package, intact and unopened, was handed over to one of the boys who rode it to a rendezvous at Salome where he turned it over to a rider come west from Yettem.

Its itinerary after that was neither known nor of interest to Gleed Stoil. The time to grab it, he said, was after it left Camp Four. "An' who the hell would be the wiser?"

"By gee," Ben said enthusiastically, "you certainly get around, Gleed! I been with this outfit better'n six months an' never even knew what become of the cattle!"

Stoil smiled remotely. "You want in?"

Appearing to give it thought, Taylor fetched the makings from a pocket and slowly curled a smoke. "What," he asked at last, "would I have to do? An' what would you be payin' for it?"

"I'm splittin' with you fifty-fifty. All you got to do is meet the Camp Four rider and relieve him of that package."

"At Salome?"

Stoil shrugged. "All I'm interested in is in getting my hands on that money. Meet him any place that suits you."

"Suppose I meet him at Salome an' he gets suspicious?"

"Be a damn good time for you to find out if you can use that gun," Stoil told him drily. "Any more questions?"

"One or two. What's to stop me, havin' met him an' gotten hold of the package, from huntin' greener pastures?"

"I don't think you will."

"Well, suppose I turn the proposition down?"

"I don't think," Stoil said, "you'll do that, either."

The silence got a little loud. The smile that curved Stoil's lips was not reflected in Stoil's eyes. "No," Ben said after a look at them, "I don't guess I will." He let the quiet ride on a spell, then: "What about the girl?"

"What about her?"

"Ain't you scared they'll get suspicious if I don't—"

"I ain't scared," Stoil said, "of anything."

Ben believed him. "No objections to me seein' her, is there?"

"I don't know of any." The Camp Three boss fished a key from his pocket, blandly handing it across. "Outside. Fourth door to the left."

"Maybe I'm dumb," Ben said, "but I don't seem to get it—I don't get it at all. Why take the risk of keeping her on your hands when you can turn her loose if—"

"That girl," Stoil said with a quick, tight grin, "is what's goin' to keep you honest. She stays right here till you hand me over that package."

Chapter Eighteen
THE BRIMMING CUP

Fargo, caught in the fury of his unleashed passions, eyed the woman with a malevolent scowl. Her rough old cheeks were loudly painted. She had her teeth in now and a big-rimmed hat with a lot of flopping foliage was jauntily clapped on her head. But there was little of jauntiness in her look. Her face was haggard and despair had written its history under her eyes.

"He's no brother to me," snarled Fargo bitterly. "He's a goddamn lyin' thief an'—"

"So the pot's calling the kettle black—"

"Never mind! He's a goddamn lyin'—Say! What are you doin' here anyway?"

"Has anyone a better right to be here than Fork Fargo's wife?"

"Fork Fargo's wife!" Mace jeered. "That's rich! What a precious comfort you must have been!" Savagely, vindictively, his hot eyes took her apart. "You got a hell of a nerve comin' 'round here now after stayin' clear all of these years."

There was regret in the misted eyes staring back at him. Her head shook slowly, sadly. "You can make a lot of mistakes in fifty-seven years and God knows I've made my share—and paid for them, too," she said. "I don't suppose I could have expected better treatment from sons like you and Reb—"

"If you rode over here to preach a sermon—"

"I came over here to warn you," Kate said gruffly. "I owe you that much, anyway. You're playing with dynamite, Mace Fargo, and you'd better stop it before you're hurt. You think you can steal this country from its rightful owners and have it all to yourself. I doubt it. Fork Fargo had that notion too, and he died in a cage like an animal. But that's not what I came to tell you. When you start crossing up a government—"

"Your solicitude is touching, Madame—"

Kate said grimly: "I'm not through. You can scoff at me, you can scoff at these Thief River ranchers, and at the Government, too, if you're that kind of fool. But I want to warn you that Ben Taylor's an agent of that government, and when you start playing games with a Taylor you're playing them for keeps. Fork Fargo tried it and his brothers tried it and they were just as smart as you—"

Mace said malignantly: "You think a lot of them goddam Taylors, don't you? Enough to let one of 'em—"

"*Mace!*"

Fargo's cheeks were dark as Kate's were white. "So it *is* true then . . . I'm just a lousy bastard.

Bad as the Fargo name stinks, I haven't any right to it . . ."

Suffused with blood, Fargo's face was twisted, bitter beyond description. The cup was running over, spilling its poison through him, relentlessly extinguishing the final spark of his vanished character.

"Damn you!" he whispered thickly. His body seemed to take on girth, to swell and stretch and quiver.

Kate tried to reason with him, to show him the end that he was shaping for himself. But her words were wasted. They were like the pearls the man scattered before swine.

"Never mind," he snarled. "You had your own life to live, you said. Damn your wanton soul! Go live it and stay out of my affairs!"

"Mace—"

"Get out!" he gritted huskily.

His eyes were like a bright hot flame.

He started toward her, slowly, inexorably, like something from a nightmare . . .

Chapter Nineteen
THE ROAD TO HELL

The march of doom through the Thief River country was irresistible as an avalanche, swift and terrible as the German *blitzkrieg*. The hour of Fargo's triumph was at hand and he was pouring all his resources into the intended complete destruction of the warring factions. Yettem's raiders had driven the smaller outfits into a program of violent reprisals aimed to reduce their supposed oppressors to a more humble status. The big owners, fearing loss of range and privilege and outraged at the extent of damage being dealt both pride and pocketbook, had banded themselves into a Committee for Public Safety and under this paraded virtue were vindictively determined to wipe the small fry out. No quarter was asked nor was any given. It was a war of extermination and all up and down the high hill country night skies flared with the roaring flames of gutted ranches. Foreclosure of his holdings drove Grierson to the squatters and they, one night under his direction, burned his entire layout. The mountains swarmed with riders, rifles cracked from brush and rimrock and it became as much as a fellow's life was worth to turn a lamp up after dark fell.

Bad as the Fargo name stinks, I haven't any right to it . . ."

Suffused with blood, Fargo's face was twisted, bitter beyond description. The cup was running over, spilling its poison through him, relentlessly extinguishing the final spark of his vanished character.

"Damn you!" he whispered thickly. His body seemed to take on girth, to swell and stretch and quiver.

Kate tried to reason with him, to show him the end that he was shaping for himself. But her words were wasted. They were like the pearls the man scattered before swine.

"Never mind," he snarled. "You had your own life to live, you said. Damn your wanton soul! Go live it and stay out of my affairs!"

"Mace—"

"Get out!" he gritted huskily.

His eyes were like a bright hot flame.

He started toward her, slowly, inexorably, like something from a nightmare . . .

Chapter Nineteen
THE ROAD TO HELL

The march of doom through the Thief River country was irresistible as an avalanche, swift and terrible as the German *blitzkrieg*. The hour of Fargo's triumph was at hand and he was pouring all his resources into the intended complete destruction of the warring factions. Yettem's raiders had driven the smaller outfits into a program of violent reprisals aimed to reduce their supposed oppressors to a more humble status. The big owners, fearing loss of range and privilege and outraged at the extent of damage being dealt both pride and pocketbook, had banded themselves into a Committee for Public Safety and under this paraded virtue were vindictively determined to wipe the small fry out. No quarter was asked nor was any given. It was a war of extermination and all up and down the high hill country night skies flared with the roaring flames of gutted ranches. Foreclosure of his holdings drove Grierson to the squatters and they, one night under his direction, burned his entire layout. The mountains swarmed with riders, rifles cracked from brush and rimrock and it became as much as a fellow's life was worth to turn a lamp up after dark fell.

Goldfield town was seized and sacked, armed raiders swarmed through Sleepy Cat, and Mesquite Flat was a patrolled camp of grim-faced, bleak-eyed riflemen. No man rode alone these days and expected to reach his destination.

Taylor's face had aged and his nerves gotten like piano strings from twenty-six hours of doing nothing in Gleed Stoil's Camp Three bailiwick. He knew pretty well what was going on from the rumors brought in by Gleed Stoil's riders and would have chanced escape but for the girl. In a fever to be gone, impatience had sharpened his temper to a razor edge and of those who ventured to speak to him, none made the mistake again. Save one—the man Stoil had set to watch him. With this fellow Ben was merely gruff, for a plan was shaping in his mind at last and the plan included his bailiff.

Ben was not a prisoner in the sense that Bella was. There were no erected walls or iron bars to cramp his whims or liberty. Within limits, he was as free to come and go as any of the Camp Three crew, but the limits were there and Ben knew them. Without a sign or word, Gleed Stoil had made them plain. Tomorrow the package from the coast was due to reach Camp Four and he was expected to intercept it before the Camp Four rider turned it over at Salome. Until that package was in Gleed Stoil's hands, Bella Hawes must remain a prisoner in Stoil's storeroom. Ben could visit her as often as he chose, but he must lock her in when he left her. It was to make sure Ben didn't forget this, Stoil had placed Tim Wyler with his sawed-off Greener just outside the door.

Night had come again when, outwardly nonchalant but inwardly tight as a clock spring, Ben drifted across to the storeroom for his fourth conversation with her.

A small lantern hung above the doorway and by its light Ben saw Wyler's mocking grin as he came up. "Playin' the bear again tonight? Chk, chk, chk! I wish I had your way with 'em," Wyler leered. "Betcha they'd need asbestos to write your memoirs on, boy."

Ben ignored him. Unlocking the thick oak door, he stepped inside, carefully closing the barrier after him. Wyler would have his ear squeezed flat against it—he always listened, but this was a thing Ben couldn't help. He could always whisper.

There was no light here so he couldn't see her face; not even now with her in his arms, with her body tight against him. She caressed his face with her finger tips, their cool touch passing like a benediction over taut cheekbones and throbbing temples. She said, trembling, "Ben—Ben, what are we going to do?"

She'd forgiven him Yettem's wife, though he hadn't said a word of her. Her faith was strong; it had come to their rescue. But it was not proof against these endless hours of duress. "There's no chance to get me out of here. You'd better go. You have your work and—"

"Shh—" he said with his lips pressed against her ear. "I've got a plan. Stoil's gone—went away this afternoon in a truck and won't be back till late, I hope. Anyway, he's gone. I'll get you loose before—"

She put a hand across his lips. "You can't! It's too risky—"

"I can," he said, "and will. Listen—" And softly, with barely moving lips, he told the plan.

"You can't!" she caught him tight. "I'll never let you, Ben—it's suicide! They'll shoot—"

"Then let 'em shoot," Ben growled. "I can do some of that myself. Remember now. In half an hour . . ." He put a key in her hand. "I'll whistle 'Ben Bolt.' Come then."

She said huskily, "This is madness! Don't do it, Ben—"

"I must."

She choked her fright against him. Fear of what he meant to try coupled to the harrowing uncertainty of these last days had broken down her barriers. She was only a woman, knowing all a woman's bodings, frustrations, griefs, alarms. She was only flesh, and flesh is weak. She clung to him and the anguished trembling of her cut him like a knife driven in his side and twisted. He ground his teeth, helpless to give her comfort, knowing he must play the hand fate dealt him—that he must do what he had to do.

She turned her tear-wet unseen face to his, tipping it upward, striving to guess what was in his eyes; but failing. "Where will all this end?"

Despair was in her tone, black as the darkness of this room; and he had no answer. He could only hold her to him with his face pressed against her hair and with his throat gone dry as desert dust. There were no words for a time like this. No words had been invented.

That half hour crawled slow as prodded snails. Ben thought he should go mad before the time for action came. But it came at last.

It lacked four minutes till the time he meant to whistle when he stepped from the cook's dark shack, carefully shutting the door behind him. Always in the past he had been cool, methodical, deliberate. Now the pounding of his pulse was like the throb of beating tom-toms and it took every ounce of willpower to throttle himself down to the appearance of an aimless saunter as he crossed the empty yard. Arrived at his objective, he dropped carelessly to a seat upon the step of the beef-packed truck parked nearest to the girl's position.

There was no one in the yard but himself and Wyler. The drivers of the trucks were in the barracks-like bunkhouse with the present members of Stoil's crew. They were playing cards and, by the sound, the drivers were stacking the money.

For a moment, as he sat down, Wyler had looked up and over at him curiously but now appeared to have relaxed back into the lethargic stupor that was his habitual state when there was no one at hand for riding.

Three minutes to go and already there was a trace of haze or something in the shadows about the cook shack. Lucky he had taken the trouble of blanketing the windows, else—

His glance snapped abruptly slanchways across the twenty feet to Wyler. The guard was half risen from his seat, crouched stiff, bent forward. He had the pose of an intent listener. But Ben knew better. The man was sniffing, was keening the breeze like a pointer. He had his head toward the cook shack. And then, across the intervening shadows, he was staring hard at Ben. And the Greener in his lap was shifted.

Two minutes; and Ben, sweat-streaked and edgy, sat motionless on that cold truck step, aware that when discovery came, Tim Wyler was going to shoot.

Flame licked up the cook shack window. Somewhere a panicked voice yelled "FIRE!" and Wyler, by the storeroom, was down upon one knee, the hollow booming of his Greener filling the night with thunder. Ben was yanking the truck door open and shouting, and cursing men were piling from the bunkhouse like ants from a burning log.

Time ran fast and the fire's flare was reaching its grotesque light across that shouting bedlam when Taylor, shrilling Ben Bolt like a fife corps, raised his head above the cab's tin armor and with one quick, sure shot dropped Wyler in his tracks.

Flashing a look across the yard, he saw the black gesticulating shapes of Stoil's crew limned against the cook shack flare; milling, helpless, they were cursing in confusion, bawling questions at one another that nobody bothered answering. They had no thought to spare the meaning of that booming Greener, no thought for its sudden silence.

A savage joy ripped Taylor's chest and, daring hope, he was reaching to snap the ignition on when the tag-end of a raking glance saw Bella, running, suddenly stumble, pitch down in a headlong fall.

With a groan he kicked the truck door open. With screaming nerves he sprinted toward her— reached her. Scooping her up in his arms he whirled and, with a prayer for luck, slowed by her added weight, he started back.

He was three feet from the truck cab's step, was daring hope once more, when a glare of swinging headlamps struck him, turning all about him bright as day.

It was Stoil returned, and he was not alone. Mouth shouting words that were lost as soon as uttered, his squat, pot-bellied shape was lumbering toward them; and on his heels came Yettem, grinning, waving a pistol in baleful glee.

Too late to stop now, Ben staggered on; shoved the girl in the cab, climbed in himself. With the switch turned on he kicked the button. Something jammed; there came no answering roar, but a thousand fissures cracked the windshield and the thump of lead on the truck's wide front was like the bounce of hail on a red tin roof.

All across the yard crouched men were advancing, guns in hand and bared teeth glinting. Stoil's bull yell came slamming forward: "Get out of that truck or I'll riddle you both!"

Having come that close, it was bitter hard to see planned victory strangled in the ashes of defeat. But hope was killed. There was no chance now.

With a bitter sigh, Ben climbed from the cab. He stood in the light with both arms raised to signify surrender. "The girl's unconscious—"

His words chopped off. He stared, bewildered, unable to credit his eyes as the foremost rustler, both hands grabbing at his stomach, crumpled suddenly and went down. To his left another with a high scared shout went skittering sideways. Then a rifle's distant, sharp, flat cracking was lashing up the echoes and Stoil's whole crew was whirling, scuttling madly for the cover of the shadows.

Ben didn't wait to see what Stoil and Yettem might do, but, with Stoil's cursing in his ears, sprang into the cab and drove a shaking boot at the stubborn starter.

The motor roared to life and they were off, were lurching across the light-sprayed yard, gathering speed as, frantically, he meshed the gears and lifted their flight from startled, half-choked snortings to the smooth, sleek whine of speed-blurred pistons.

They were off, without lights and with Stoil's crashing rifles back of them. Lead pummeled the truck, but Ben held his foot to the floorboards and they went rocketing down the black road like an uncoupled freight car on a forty-mile grade. Barring accidents, they were free and Ben wasn't minded to stop for anything.

He switched on his lights with a vote of thanks to the unknown rifleman who had snatched this victory from wreckage. But for that man he might now be dead and Bella . . .

"Ben! Where are we?" she cried suddenly, sitting up.

"We're headed home—"

"We really made it?"

He asked anxiously, "Are you all right, Bella? That fall—"

"I'm all right."

Then suddenly Taylor, rounding a rocky shoulder where the footslopes of the Lapaz Mountains make their leftward toboggan slanting toward the plains, jammed on the brakes, dragging their hurtling beef-packed vehicle to a lesser velocity, bringing it to a grinding, jerky stop. The statue holding the center of the road dissolved, became a living, grinning horseman who doffed his hat with exaggerated gallantry, came reining his gelding over, laughing at them, chiding them. "That all you got to say to Santa Claus?"

Ben said: "Steve, how did you get here?"

"Oh, the bronc leaped a couple mountains. What'd you think of that shootin'? Not so bad for hand-spanked work, eh? Didn't even have a telescope—"

"So that was you, was it?" Ben said thinly. "You certainly get around. I expect you sent those telegrams by airmail or—"

"Well, no," Steve Fontana confessed. "I . . . er—I didn't send 'em. I took a look at 'em an' it kinda seemed to me like—like—"

"Well, like—what?"

"You recollect tellin' me about how Fargo had grabbed off Bella? Well, I got to thinkin' about it an' about how brash you could be when somethin' got you riled enough, an' I says to myself, I says: 'Steve, ol' boy, your pard's goin' to ride smack-dab into a trap sure as God makes little green apples!' It seemed to me like it would be a heap more important for all concerned if I sort of jogged along in your wake a spell an'—"

"It did, eh?" Ben's voice bit like frosty ice. "So you thought lookin' after me was a heap more important than—"

"Ben!"

"I'll take care of this," Ben said, shaking off her hand. "God, Steve—I thought I could depend on you—thought you were a guy to ride the river with. I thought—"

"Yeah. I reckon," Steve said, "I'm jest one of them guys they pave the road to hell with. But..."

"But?" snarled Taylor. "Damn it, Steve, there *ain't* no buts! You've killed the only chance we had of stoppin' that rustled beef short of the coast! You've—Oh, hell. Get in," he muttered thickly.

"Mebbe," Steve said, "I—"

"Don't argue!"

Fontana disengaged his rifle, patted the horse's neck affectionately. "So long, ol' boy; take care of yourself." He looped the reins about the saddle horn, sharply slapped the animal's rump. He walked around the truck then, opening the door on Bella's side. By the time he'd glumly settled on the seat the truck was rolling, diving savagely down the long descent that led to the plain's dark void.

Chapter Twenty
BURNED BRIDGES

It was pretty late when Fargo reached the roadhouse—designedly so. But if he had hoped to find it dark and without custom, the hope was doomed. The sprawling, ramshackle structure was a blaze of light. Fargo's face at the sight got a little darker, possibly, the glint of his eyes more brash. But he did not stop nor slow his horses' progress till he reached the roadhouse rack. Getting down then, he loosely knotted the led-horse's reins, tossed his own across the rail and with a quick, hard look about him, grimly strode inside.

The Portuguese swamper had the barroom to himself.

"What's the idea burning all these lights?" asked Fargo curtly.

The swamper shrugged and went on with his work till Fargo, reaching out, spun him around. "Damn you! When I speak I want an answer!"

"Lady worried."

"Lady . . . ?" Gone still, Mace Fargo stared, suspicious. "What lady?"

"No sabe."

"Guest?"

"Yes. Guest lady. Got little girl."

"Where are they?"

"In other room." The swamper gestured toward the back. Leaning on his mop then, he looked at Fargo curiously. "What you want? You want drink?"

"This woman," Fargo said. "Is she asleep? I mean, has she gone to bed?"

"No go to bed. Go worry."

"What's she worried about?"

"Boss Kate. She go away. No come back."

"I see." Fargo's glance, turned thoughtful, passed a look about the room. That look rested longest on the opened bottle, the part-filled glass that stood in a ring of wetness on the bar. "Tell her to come out here. I want to talk to her."

The swamper looked a little dubious. "Maybe—"

"Go on—tell her!"

With a Latin shrug, the man leaned his mop against the bar and shuffled off, passing through a door at the room's far end and knocking upon some farther, unseen barrier.

Stepping casually to the bar, Fargo leaned an elbow on it. That half-filled glass seemed to hold strange fascination for him. He gave it an absorbed interest till the slap of sandals heralded his messenger's return. He looked up then and his glance was bright as the crystals of the chandelier.

The woman who followed the swamper in was

young. Blue of eye she was, with black bobbed hair worn page-boy fashion and features that still held trace of an earlier piquancy despite the bruises care had painted beneath her eyes. She said: "You're the man who wished to speak to me?"

Her level glance held signs of doubt. There was in it the suggestion he'd mistaken her for another. But when he nodded the woman's eyes, no longer bothering to hide their trouble, narrowed. "My husband sent you here?"

"I don't know your husband, madam," Fargo said a little stiffly. "Is he a native of this—"

"He's a cattle thief. He calls himself Ace Yettem."

Fargo's back went hard against the bar. Distrust, bright and hot, was in the look he stabbed across at her. "That sounds a little harsh," he said, "comin' from a fellow's wife. You're not serious—?"

"Do you know where—" She broke off to stare at him intently. "You're his brother, aren't you?"

Fargo's brows drew blackly down. "No!" he snarled through lips squeezed tight. "I've no connection with the b—with the fellow—no connection whatsoever! *Do you hear me?*"

"Of course I hear you. You don't have to shout."

Flushed, still scowling, Fargo pulled himself together. "Sorry," he said gruffly. "I'm easy riled tonight. There's been murder done. This country's getting so a man ain't safe to stick his head outside the door." He said more calmly: "You related to the woman—" He stopped to rub a hard, bright stare across the swamper's face. He said to him, "That all you got to do?" and waited till the man, reluctantly, picked up his pail and mop and left.

Fargo said then, "You related to the woman who runs this joint?"

"Kate Stalleon? Yes—by marriage. My husband's right name is Fargo. Kate's his mother."

It must have hit Fargo hard, that knowledge in another's hands. But if it did, the fact was not evident—not unless you were keen enough to count that statue-stillness, that bright intensity of glance.

He said bleakly, "Then I've bad news for you. Kate Stalleon's dead. Strangled by a rope. I found her dangling from a tree beside the Mesquite road. She's on her horse outside."

The face of Yettem's wife went white as wood-ash. She stared at him with eyes dilated, horrified.

Fargo said: "My name is Hockaday. If you see the sheriff or any of his deputies, I wish you'd report this for me. I intended doing it myself, but I've unexpected business to attend that can't well wait."

She nodded mutely.

"Tell him just what I've said. That I was

coming to town and found her dangling from a limb along the Mesquite road. I cut her down, found her horse—which, luckily, hadn't strayed far—tied her across the saddle and brought her in."

He watched her for a moment consideringly, as though he'd something else to say, was wondering how to put it. What he did say, finally, gruffly, was: "I suppose this is quite a shock to you—be a shock to everyone, I guess. This is a pretty tough country . . . a lot too brutal for a woman. With the kind of riffraff ridin' these hills today, a woman's not safe one holy minute; only three-four days ago some girl was kidnapped." He said gruffly: "In your place, Mrs. Yettem, I'd get out of it."

He bowed curtly, wheeled and went out of the place.

Something fluttered palely against the darkness of the veranda flooring. Arrested, he was stooping to pick it up when a pistol's near explosion broke the silence into fragments. That sudden stooping was all that saved his life. The bullet's wind was cold against his neck and memory of that half-filled glass beside the bottle on the bar shoved his stomach against the floorboards and smashed a raking hand to a stretched and rigid stop beyond his head. Like that he waited, with his lips peeled back and with his brash stare savagely probing the stirred-up shadows by the horses.

Patience was rewarded. There came the creak of hung-up leather and a snorting horse stepped sideways and Fargo fired—fired till the gun was empty, then trotted forward, reloading the weapon and holding it ready, half minded to use it again even though there be no need. And there wasn't; his first look at the crumpled shape told him that.

Callously he kicked the body over and struck a match the better to see by. It was Ide—Monk Ide. Recognition made a whistling curse of Fargo's breath and he kicked the corpse again and, swearing, got astride his horse and went larruping off to the south.

Chapter Twenty-one
HOG WILD

Taylor drove steadily, stopping only when he had to stop, for gasoline and coffee. There was little talking, no one being in the mood for it. They drew what sustenance they could from occasional candy bars and sandwiches. Off and on, Steve and Bella dozed, but Ben stuck doggedly to the wheel with bloodshot eyes set dead ahead, with stiff, beard-stubbled cheeks grimly locking away his thoughts.

Night fled. The sun came up and the day grew hot and the stubs of Steve's smoked cigarettes grew steadily more noticeable underfoot, and always the motor's high grinding hum beat its senseless tune against their ears, and the hot oil's smell made a ceaseless stench and the views thrust up by unreeling miles became old stories before they were born and sun's glare off the polished road was a steady misery to aching eyes that were tired of watching the mountains crawl by.

They nooned at Wittman, if one could so describe the purchase of three box lunches and beer. While Bella went on this shopping spree and Steve took care of the gassing of the truck, the oil, the water, and air for the tires, Ben sent off the telegrams he'd three days ago given Fontana. Rewriting the one to Headquarters he described the trucks he'd seen at Camp Three, advising their stopping at Beaumont, which had an airport and could be gotten to in time. To this report he appended a thumbnail sketch of affairs at Thief River—so far as he knew them—and, hustling back to the station, found Steve with his lunch half eaten chuckling over something with Bella. He noted with tightening lips how their laughter slacked off with his coming; but made no comment. It was the price of his outburst at Steve.

Steve said: "I'll drive while you eat, if you like," and Ben nodded.

The day wore on and the drone of the motor was like a drug. They had figured about what the truck could do, how much that speed would be cut by traffic and by the slowing of their pace while passing through the occasional towns that sprawled like upended packing-boxes along the concrete ribbon of their way; and by this figuring could determine approximately where they were at any given time. But the hands of Ben's watch appeared to turn through glue, and Thief River, like Sheridan in the poem, seemed ever to be endless miles away.

As with Ben, time with Mace Fargo had become at once both an endless and a precious thing.

Precious in that each passing moment the events he'd set in motion were bringing him inexorably closer to the fruits of his planned victory, or—

And that was what made time drag so. The damnable uncertainty attending such a venture, the suspense with its inevitable havoc to nerves stretched already to the breaking point, the unpredictability of the human element in this thing, the fear that some factor vital to success might not have received its proper share of his attention— might even have been overlooked completely.

A kind of dread had seized him, dread traceable to the night of Kate Stalleon's visit—the first she had ever paid him . . . and the last. That visit had been the start of it and Ide's attempted drygulching of him had done little to bolster his confidence in the men he must depend on. If Ide would double-cross him, why not the others? What more had they to gain than Ide? Was the man's treachery an omen—forerunner of general mutiny?

From the start he'd held no illusions concerning his lieutenants' allegiance should events transpire to make it seem he could not cut this; his knowledge of the human equation under such conditions had been one of the deciding reasons why he'd geared the machinery for this stunt to the pattern that he had—that interlocking pattern of secrecy which had kept the left hand in ignorance of the doings of the right. Yes, he'd known very well what would happen were the end of this venture ever allowed to appear doubtful.

Bitter irony! There was no taint of doubt—not a shadow. Success was within his grasp. Another eight hours would see him the strongest force in Thief River; he'd be owning the country from end to end. Already the biggest owners were bankrupt, or without further means of promoting the fight, or were ranchless, or horseless, or stripped of their men. The two-bit spreads were deteriorated or decimated into mere wandering bands of guerrillas. In all this high hill region there was not a force that could stand against him—or would not be eight hours hence. And yet—and though he would not admit it—Mace Fargo was afraid.

This was dread's grim power, dread's corrosive influence. It could change a man from a state of arrogant confidence to the wretchedness of shivering despair, could drag him from the top down into the nethermost of depths; could drop him from success to failure. It had not done this to Fargo, but it was at work.

He'd been unafraid when he'd turned that night to find Kate Stalleon standing in the doorway; had still been unafraid when she had left. But something had got to working on him during that journey to the roadhouse. Not conscience, certainly, for his acts showed that he had none.

Perhaps it was some aspect of religion, of those beliefs handed down by generations of his kind. Perhaps it was mixed up with superstition. At any rate, from that time on the dread had hold of him, a hold that steadily, inexorably, was being tightened. It was a conviction—conviction of disaster.

There was nothing in actual fact to give him reason for that certainty; little things, perhaps—it was these that he was counting, but nothing in itself that was important. First there was Kate Stalleon's visit, her revelations, and her death. Then came Monk Ide's treachery, his own distrust of Yettem and of Yettem's limitations, the risk they all were running by their holding of Bella Hawes. There was Yettem's wife, the dangerous knowledge she was holding; his impersonation of Hockaday and Hockaday's subsequent disappearance. These were the things that gnawed at him, the things his conviction fed upon.

He was thinking of these things now as he tramped about the ranch house, restless, irritable, balked and mean. They had gotten beneath his guard, these things; had undermined his confidence. He could not shake off their premonition of evil. It was like a hangman's rope about his neck, it tampered with his breathing; and when the phone rang suddenly, he stood like a man who had Death's hand upon his shoulder. His own hand shook as Yettem's voice came over the miles. Yettem said:

"Bett Tanter's dead—I just got word; Grierson shot him on the street in Goldfield. They've slapped Grierson in the jug, but that ain't bringin' our law back. Look! You better get busy quick 'fore some guy's shoved in we can't control—an' look: I got some more bad news. Taylor's been out here stringin' Stoil—I'm at Camp Three—an' last night he busted the girl loose an' they've got away in one of our trucks! Yeah. A loaded one. I've decked the rest of 'em out with new tags an' papers an' I've had 'em repainted, but—"

"Taylor—" Fargo muttered. "Taylor an' the girl . . . you say they've gone?" His voice was choked, was husky, shaky. "Where—?"

"Headed for Thief River last we saw of 'em. I think Fontana's with 'em—we found his bronc turned loose in the hills, an'—uh—Wait a minute—"

The receiver slipped from Fargo's hand. He leaned against the wall with all his muscles sagging. His haggard cheeks were the color of parchment and his mouth was twisted, gone awry. He saw his cattle empire crumpling; all his dreaded fears were realized. He did not see the things about him in this room. It were as though no walls were there. The things his stare bit at and through were not so much as a mist across the nightmare vision he had of all that he had worked for, all he'd lied and killed and burned for, crashing in a tumbling chaos of broken shards about his feet. This was the beginning of the end; Monk Ide had said it—the writing was on the wall. That the Thief River feud was going the way he'd planned it meant nothing—meant less than nothing. It gave but an empty shell to victory: an appearance; and *he knew* what appearances were worth!

They were licked. The bite had been too big, the conception too rosily painted. The money from that last haul hadn't reached his hands; the man who'd ridden it yesterday from Camp Four was gone—vanished like the pot of gold that lay by the rainbow's end. They were licked and it was time to claw for the saddle. The pattern was breaking, that great and intricate organization he had so carefully built was cracking up, was melting—melting as the high-crag snow melts under the blaze of sun. The winds of retribution were on the loose and it was time to ride—to ride before the gods of vengeance struck; for all ahead was chaos . . . chaos and fury and vengeance, with himself at the end of a rope.

Security was gone; with his own hand he had banished it, had proclaimed gun law, and it was gun law that would come for him. He must not wait! If this Thief River crowd ever learned what he'd been up to, they would tear him limb from limb! His bubble of empire was burst and shattered, was acrunch beneath his feet, but there was still life—if he could save it. *He must ride!*

He threw the receiver back on its hook, and in his office, atremble with haste, dug his profits from the safe. Bank's currency. He'd had the foresight to build his horde of large-denomination bills, a fortune easily stowable about his person.

He stuffed his pockets, strapped a bulging money belt beneath his shirt. But as he moved about, preparing for this flight, the things he'd learned from Yettem kept dinning through his mind. Gone was that fine great kingdom he had dreamed of—gone! And Taylor—damn him!—had wrought this havoc! Taylor—his part brother! The man was a fool for luck—it seemed impossible he could have found and entered Camp Three, much more so that he could have gotten clear with Bella. But he had done it—Yettem said so; claimed that even now the two of them were speeding toward Thief River with a truckload of stolen beef! That evidence—

With a bitter oath Fargo whirled as once more the wall phone blared. "Damn the thing! Let the—" He thought of something and changed his mind. Pulling himself together he took down the receiver. "Fargo speaking."

It was Yettem again.

"For Chrissake," Yettem growled, "Don't go hangin' up till I'm through! I've found out where that 'brand fluid' went—Stoil got it! Yes—*Stoil!*

Jumped the guy that was ridin' it to Salome. Knocked him over the head—Sure I got it! What the hell did you think I called you for? I got it right in my britches pocket an' Stoil's all through with his goddamn tricks! Now look—you want I should send it on or—"

"No." Inspired, Fargo said: "Hang right onto it and stay where you are. I'm comin' up that way in a couple days an' I'll pick it up. Take over Stoil's job till I can send someone out to replace him."

He hung up then with a tight, sly grin. He'd use Yettem this one last time, and then . . . He chuckled. They might have him on the skids, but there was plenty sting yet in the old snake's spit, and they'd damned well be finding it out!

It was time to ride, all right; and he was going to ride. Now was the time to get out of this—now, before the reckoning came.

But there were one or two things he meant to do before shaking the dust of this damn country from his heels. One or two . . .

He smiled a private smile, lean and thin like the smirk of a wolf.

From the wall he lifted down the new gun gotten by special order from Springfield, Massachusetts—the rifle that held eight slugs and released them all like one, if you kept your finger hard on the trigger. He hadn't had a chance to try it out yet and was halfway glad that he hadn't.

He would make its christening an occasion. He would use it to get Ben Taylor.

Oh, yes! He'd be there when the truck came in!

And he was. All set and ready.

It was exactly four by the fly-speckled clock back of Wolters' bar when Mace and his foreman, Ed Kreel, got down from their broncs and went into the store for a drink.

Fargo had the new rifle under his arm and had a couple drinks while they talked its points over with Wolters. They took a bottle then and adjourned to a table by the window. The glass was coated with dust, but they could see enough of the street for their purpose.

They didn't talk much. After they killed the bottle, Fargo ordered supper. Kreel didn't seem very hungry, but Fargo ate with an enthusiasm that won Wolters' grudging approval. They had several cups of black coffee. Kreel called for another bottle.

After a while, when it began to get dark, Wolters suggestively wound up the clock, but the hint went by unheeded. He fidgeted around, cleaned the bar again, shifted some of the stock on the grocery side, meantime eyeing them covertly.

"Gettin' kind of late," he said, clearing his throat.

Fargo turned half around in his chair and the look he leveled at Wolters left the man's cheeks gray as driftwood. Kreel said: "You needn't wait on us. If you got something on your mind, get at it; we'll take care of your customers."

Jerking a nod, muttering something about some brew he had to see to, Wolters eased himself out of their company, departing through a door at the back.

It was not long afterwards that Kreel, carrying a drink to his mouth, abruptly tensed with the lifting glass paused level with his chin. The high far whine of driving pistons stilled their breathing.

Truck sound!

A cold, thin grin licked Fargo's lips. Rising, he picked up the rifle, and Kreel, setting down his drink untasted, followed him from the store.

In the deep, banked shadows of the junipers they stood and watched the truck roll into town. They heard its brakes screech in protest, saw it slow to a grating stop before the hotel porch. A man got out—Fontana; they knew him by his shortness, by the way he held his shoulders. They heard him say: "Well, that's the way it was, an' my bein' sorry, I guess, ain't goin' to change it. If there's anything I can do . . . Well, O. K. Good night. Night, Bella."

They watched him stride corralwards, the sound of his crunching bootsteps loud in the late night quiet; and the creak of leather as he strapped gear on a horse came plainly to them, and the gentle run of the animal's hoofs as it took him up into the hills. Then all was still again and, had they not known better, had they not heard him talking to someone in it, they would have thought the truck was empty.

The strain of waiting appeared to hit Kreel hardest. He kept shifting his weight about, kept fiddling with things about his person, hitching at his cartridge belt and puffing out his breath in irritated, patently exasperated sighs. But Fargo stood rock still, his dim-seen face wreathing a wintry kind of pleasure as he leaned, quite patient, on his rifle.

Then that rifle was lifting, settling gently against his shoulder as the noise of an opening truck door brushed harsh sound against the shadows. Kreel, looking, saw the girl climb out and, after her, Taylor. Saw them pause, heard Taylor's voice and the girl's voice, sharper, make reply; then she was crossing the glare of the headlamps, gone, and Taylor was limned against them.

The swift staccato roar of Fargo's rifle split the night wide open.

Taylor spun three-quarters around and pitched face downward in the dust.

Before the shock-rooted, stricken girl could move Fargo's grip was on her arm and he was rushing her, Kreel ahead of them, toward where the slatted lines of the pole corral showed whitely in the truck lights.

Then Hawes' strident fright-pitched voice was shouting, "Stop! Get away from those horses—My God! *Bella!*" And he was running after them, panting, cursing, sobbing all at once.

They stopped. "Hold her," Fargo muttered, and shoved the girl at Kreel. Turning, scowling, he took the pistol from his armpit and, aiming with deliberate care, coldly dropped Hawes in his tracks.

An oath fell out of Kreel's slack jaw and Bella screamed, and Fargo, whirling, struck her hard across the mouth. "Hold her, damn you!" he cursed at Kreel. "All right, then, *carry* her if you got to. We—*Here!* Wait! What the hell we foolin' 'round with horses for when there's a truck back there all ready to go? *Come on!*"

Chapter Twenty-two
JUMPED SADDLES

Ben came to, to find Fontana bending over him, to find his shoulders backed by Steve Fontana's knee. Fontana's face was a pale-seen blur that seemed, somehow, to hold a look of fright; and the restive stamping of Fontana's horse, the tinkle of its bit chains, were the only sounds that Ben could hear.

He said, "What the hell happened?" and struggled to get up. But Steve held him firmly. "Take it easy, boy—take it *easy,*" Steve said gruffly. "Ain't had no chance to look you over yet; I—"

"Thought you'd gone—"

"I come back all right when I heard that rifle—"

"Rifle?" Then Ben noticed that the truck was gone; and suddenly his mind was crystal-clear and he said: "Bella—"

"Steady, boy. This is gonna be tough," Steve muttered. "They've got her—grabbed her an' gone off again—Kreel an' Fargo—*Here!* Hold on! You got to—"

But Ben seemed suddenly strong as six. Fontana couldn't hold him. Ben shoved him off, came snarling to his feet. "The truck—"

"They've took the truck, boy."

"If you saw 'em," gritted Taylor, "why the hell didn't you stop 'em?"

"I didn't see 'em. I was damn near up to Keeler's—halfway to Tortilla Flat, when I heard that rifle. Sounded like one of them Tommy-guns an' I come tearin' back. Wasn't nobody here but you an' old Hawes—an' him jest barely gaspin'—"

"Where is he now?"

"Kicked off. Fargo drilled him through the guts. Look here, boy—" Fontana swallowed, slewed from the blaze of Taylor's eyes. "If only we could round us up some—"

"Come on!" Ben snarled. "Rope out a string of them horses . . ." He staggered, would have fallen had not Steve grabbed him.

"Now you set down," Steve muttered, "an' lemme get a look at that hole. You been shot up, boy."

Ben wouldn't sit but stood scowling and impatient in Hawes' living room while Fontana got a lamp lit, brought towels and water in a basin. "Cold," Steve said, "but I reckon it's better than nothin'. Hold still now an' lemme look . . . Mmmm . . . Don't see how he come to miss . . . All you got's a scratch, boy." He ran an exploring finger along the gouge above Ben's left ear. "Hurt?"

Taylor's white cheeks were set and stubborn.

"You lost a lot of blood. I don't reckon—"

"Get on with it," Taylor gritted. "Slap a rag on it an' quit jawin'!"

"Hell, you can't go chasin' after them birds in your cond—"

Ben jerked loose of him, started for the door. Steve grabbed him. "Wait, you golrammed idjit—"

"Give me that towel!" Taylor snatched it, sloshed it around his head, and twisted the ends in. "By God, if Fargo don't hang for this, I—"

"He's goin' to take a deal of catchin', boy."

"I'll catch him," Ben said grimly, "if it's the last damn thing I do!"

Chapter Twenty-three
WORLD WITHOUT END

"Snap out of it, boy! Wake up! Wake up!"

With one hand clutching the wheel and his blue eyes squinted against the road glare, Fontana shook Ben Taylor from his slumber. Ben groaned, grumpily shrank away from Fontana's reach; but Steve was adamant. "Come out of it, boy! Get your eyes open—this here's Beaumont!"

"Beau . . . Oh, hell." With a final groan Ben sat up, stretching out his long-cramped legs, gouging the sleep from his eyes. "God, but I feel awful! Mouth tastes like a garbage can—Did you say this was Beaumont?" He scowled through the bug-smeared windshield. "Don't look like Beaumont to me."

"Outskirts—we're cuttin' in from the north. Detour. They got 70 closed. Guys workin' on it. Where'd you want to stop?"

"I want to send a wire. Look for a Western Union."

Quarter to ten had seen them leaving Thief River last night on a string of Hawes' fast horses. Ben had a pretty fair idea where Fargo was headed; this open seizure of Bella spelled just one thing to Taylor—flight. Fargo was on the run; and in all this land, Ben thought, there was just one place where there could be any safety for him. Aboard one of those German freighters that was transporting Thief River beef! Once let him reach it and hope was done for; they'd see neither him nor Bella again. But if they could head him off...

As the chase strung out, Ben became more and more convinced his guess was a good one; the fugitives were headed westward toward California and the coast, and by the shortest route available: U.S. 70.

Cross-countrying on Hawes' horses, Ben and Steve thundered into Apache Junction at ten minutes past eleven, only to learn that a Bengal Transport truck—the kind that Fargo was driving—had come through a half hour earlier off State 88 and headed west. They yanked a deputy from his poker game long enough to get the use of a car. Leaving their horses in his care, they'd sputtered off, but two miles east of Mesa the old crock gave a long sad sigh and quit. Shank's Mare got them into Mesa but lost them precious time—time that might well make all the difference in the world to Bella; and further time was lost getting hold of another car. But they got one finally and came clanking into Phoenix on a flat at seventeen minutes to one. Taylor acted like a madman. He cursed the under-sheriff up one side and down the other during the twenty-five minutes of red tape insisted on by that officer before he'd consent to get them a car; but when he finally did, it was a good one that Ben signed for—a long and streamlined Cord.

The chase began in earnest.

All went well until they got to Hope; brief inquiries at Alhambra, Wittman, Wickenburg and Wendon elicited the information that a Bengal truck was someplace ahead of them. But Hope did not recollect seeing any such vehicle—or a recent truck of any kind, for that matter. More time was lost and, at Quartzsite, still more. No one there could remember the recent passing of a Bengal truck; there had been several trucks of the closed van type, but none with the Bengal name on. "Come on!" snarled Taylor in a fever of impatience. "We're on the right track—we got to be! They're headin' for Kolbrook's on the coast—Fargo means to board one of those ships, an' if he ever makes it . . ."

His face was gray and twisted. Steve could guess what thoughts and fears, what reproaches were driving his partner on; what it would mean to Ben if his hunch should prove a wrong one or, proving right, if Fargo should get away. There'd be no rest in life for him; there'd be—

Steve said: "Couldn't you wire for help? Send a—"

"Goin' to. Goin' to wire headquarters. We got to play every card we got, Steve." Ben's voice was husky. "We *got* to stop him!"

"Guess there'd be no place for you in the Service if—"

"Hell with the Service—think what it would mean to *Bella* . . . God! Can't you ring more speed outta this crate?"

Steve did his best. Shortly after noon, he was considerably relieved to find Ben fallen into an exhausted sleep. Taylor had said, "We'll wire from Beaumont," and Steve bent all his energies into getting there.

Then Beaumont was all around them and Steve was braking the Cord to a curve. "This is it," he said. "There's your Western Union. I'll jump across the street an' get us somethin' to chew on an' gargle—"

"Make it snappy," Ben said. "This won't take a minute."

It did, though; it took six. There were other people in the office, a fat man and a woman, and the woman had to argue with the clerk. When Ben's turn came, the clerk looked up from his form to say: "You could use a course in writing, brother. Is this," he pointed, " 'Klotax'? . . . Yeah? All right; I'll read this back so there won't be no mistake. You'd be surprised at the dumb—"

Ben's groan combined despair with fury. "I'm in a hurry, guy!"

The clerk took another look at him and got down to business. " 'Order Coast Guard cutter,' " he read, " 'rushed to point opposite Kolbrook San

Onofre estate. Stand by 500 yards off shore and watch for blinker signal. Three long, six short, three long. Taylor.' "

"Right—"

"Will there be an answer?"

"No," Ben snarled, and tossing the fellow a crumpled bill, bolted savagely for the street. Steve was in the car with coffee and cold sandwiches. Ben slid under the wheel, stamped the motor into life, and again the chase was on.

"We'll cut over onto 395," he muttered, eating as he drove. "That'll get us far as Elsinore. After that we'll have to take State 74, I guess—according to the map that's the shortest way of gettin' there. God! if we can only make it!"

"How far we got to go?"

"To Kolbrook's? Another sixty-seventy miles—"

"Say!" Steve cried. "What the hell we foolin' with this crock for? They got a airport in this town!"

"Good Christ! Where is it?" Ben said breathlessly.

"Other end of town—we passed it comin' in. I never thought—"

"Pray for luck!" Ben gritted and screeched a U-turn square in the face of traffic.

Far ahead, and beneath them, light dug a pinpoint of radiance from the gloom of shadows swirled up by the fall of dusk. Their pilot pointed, turned and shouted something which the wind tore out of his mouth. Then something happened to one of the motors; it started missing and the ship's nose fell away before them in a dive that took them downward at a velocity that made Steve's hair curl. The point of light rushed up at them like a blazing torch. But just as it seemed they must dash themselves to pieces, with motors stilled and wind whistling through the wires like a shrieking maniac, the plane leveled off in a kind of buzzard circle and Ben discovered with a gasp of horror that the radiance below was caused by the flare from flaming buildings. Then suddenly there was nothing under them but the cold dark flash of water. The world stood on its head and the monstrous pier slammed up at them like something out of Burroughs.

There was a jolt—another that seemed to shake the plane from end to end. The pier—a flash of wood—was under them and they were skimming down it at incredible speed, headed directly for the flames. Miraculously they sped straight through them and, bumping around in a great half circle, stopped.

Ben was out on the ground in an instant, sprinting for the burning boathouse with Steve not a pace behind. The structure roared with a gleeful fury and heat was like a furnace breath and nothing human moved anyplace in sight. The boathouse seemed abandoned to its fate. Through gusts of smoke wind-driven across the shore, Ben could see flames' brightness licking up the nearer pilings of Kolbrook's million-dollar pier. Then, blinded by flames and smoke, Ben's feet struck something soft and yielding, and he was tripping, pitching forward in a rolling headlong fall.

He came up on his elbows, clawed to his feet and whirled to find Steve bending over something black and crumpled that groaned, that whimpered as Fontana turned it over. A man—Norman Kolbrook; though the picture king was scarcely recognizable beneath that bloody grime. He'd been shot; been practically riddled by something high-powered and terrible. He was nearly gone. It was cause for wonder that he breathed at all.

Dropped to a squat beside Fontana, Ben put an ear to those painfully moving lips. "Fargo—" they whispered. "Fargo . . . rendezvous with freighter . . . miles due west—"

A sigh came out of Kolbrook then and Ben stood back, convinced the man was gone. But he wasn't, quite. Fontana bent suddenly forward and then thoughtfully straightened to his feet. He swung a puzzled look at Taylor. "Couldn't get it. Something about 'quick firer'—"

"That's a gun," Ben grunted. "Probably on the cruiser they been using to tow the beef lighters out to the freighters. Fargo's grabbed it—taken it for his getaway. Him an' Kolbrook must've squabbled. Mace set this place afire to burn the flotilla and stop pursuit. Dammit," he scowled out across the sea, "d'you suppose Kolbrook meant the spot he picks up the freighter is however-many-miles-it-is *due west?* From here?" He held cupped palms about his eyes, but the sea was black and only the nearest waves caught shape and color from the fire. For a second he thought to catch the dim far flutter of motors, but he could not be certain. The noise of the breakers—the sound of the flames, was too close, too loud.

"Where's that cutter?" Steve began. "Do you—"

His last words, those. The rest were lost in the crash of a shell beside the pier. Planking flew. Splinters, gouged from the pier by fragments of bursting shell, filled the air with their savage whirring and Ben, yanking a tiny one from his cheek, swung around to find Steve bloody and motionless, sprawled with his face in the sand.

"Don't be a . . . fool!" Steve gasped as Ben, cursing, sank beside him. "Never mind me . . . Get—get after 'em, boy . . . Get Bella—"

Ben gripped him hard, but life was gone. The Call had come and Steve had answered.

Ben stumbled to his feet. Jaws clenched and no shame in him for the mist that fogged his gaze, he sprinted for the dark bulk that marked their grounded plane. "No luck," the pilot grunted, scowling up from where he tinkered with the left wing motor. "We're here for quite a spell—"

Ben lurched away. He put his hat across Steve's face and stared bleak-eyed across the dark and swirling waters that separated him from Kolbrook's unseen, fleeing cruiser. Cold, unbroken black, the ocean loomed like Ben's own future were the rest of his life to be lived with Bella out of it. Where *was* that blasted cutter?

Ten minutes fled with the sea still black, and then with an eerie suddenness light came sweeping across the wave crests. Searchlight's glare! Bright, then black, then bright again. A cutter's riding lights came out of the murk, rounded a jutting point and came curling in toward the flame-lit shore. Stopped. Hung and tossed five hundred yards away.

Ben's flash in feverish hands blinked out its message, signed it. An answering flash bit back at him. The cutter's lights moved forward and Ben sprinted for the pier. If only they were in time! If only—

He sprang as the fenders bumped.

A blond young guy with florid face and an Ensign's stripes was in command. He listened to Ben's story with an amazed, shocked, stare, and then: "By George!" he snapped, "Do they expect to get away with that? The curs! I'll blow that tub from the water, sir!"

"But you can't!" Ben cried. "You're forgetting the girl—she's aboard it with the rest of them!"

• • •

Aboard the cruiser, locked in the cabin where Mace Fargo had confined her, Bella had listened to the bitter quarrel on the deck outside with mixed emotions. Yettem was insisting that she be allowed to remain in the cruiser when he and Fargo left it to board the German freighter—that much of the argument she had heard and understood. That his reasons had no foundation of altruism she was well aware. Yettem was scared. She complicated things. "Do you think," Fargo had snarled in a fury, "I'm goin' to let her go at this late date? I'll see her in hell before I'll see her back with Taylor!"

There'd been much more of it, much more of it and not all of it by any means concerned with Bella. Then there had come a sudden cry—Yettem's fright-filled shriek—a splash; and, hardly knowing what she did or why she did it, Bella had snatched a life belt down and thrust it through the porthole, hoping that Yettem would get it.

She was still half numb with reaction from the things she'd been through. She had no knowledge of Fargo's intentions, save only that he was bolting and was determined she should share his flight and exile. That it would be a life of degradation she could not doubt. Yet she was not afraid—her thoughts were not on the future. Her mind was still too numb with the shock of seeing Ben and her father shot like dogs before her to be concerned as yet with worries for herself. She kept seeing Ben in the glare of the truck's bright lights as he had spun to that rifle's crashing, had pitched forward into the street's gray dust.

What was there to live for? She had asked the question a hundred times during the hours she'd passed with Fargo. But life is strong in all of us and hope never wholly dies. Perhaps, she thought, one of them still lives. Her father, possibly; there could be no chance for Ben—no man could live through the withering blast that had belched from Fargo's rifle. But a pistol shot, unless dead center, need not necessarily prove fatal—

She stiffened to the sound of Fargo's booted feet. He was coming down the companionway, was stopping before her cabin. She heard the grate of a key in the lock.

She backed till her legs were against the bunk. Fargo was before her, grinning—stripping her with his willful glance; mocking the pallor of her cheeks, malicious, gloating.

"The freighter's not here. We've got to wait—" He stopped talking suddenly, closed the space between them at a stride and grabbed her roughly. She was like a board in his arms, but she was *in* his arms and could not get away. His breath was hot against her cheek. "You're goin' to make the waitin' pleasant—"

He laughed huskily as she broke into fierce,

violent resistance. This was child's play to a man of his rugged build and he enjoyed it; leering, confident of the outcome, knowing he would have his way. He had always wanted to feel her writhing body squeezed like this against him. "Too good for me, are you?" He ripped the neckline of her dress away, jerked it down across a shoulder. "Let's see about that!"

With the cutter proceeding at half speed west Taylor stood with the Ensign at the bridge. There was no light showing but the binnacle, and the helmsman's shape blotted that out.

"Voice off the bow," came the lookout's call. "Cry for help! He's in the water—"

"Full speed astern!"

Ben could feel the cutter losing way, heard the creak of davits as a boat was lowered. He was at the rail when the boat came back and a dripping figure came up the rope and stood before them, white and shaking, with a dangling life belt clutched in his hands as though meaning never to let loose of it—Yettem! The man's brash eyes gleamed as he met Ben's stare. "I'll talk," he growled; and did, confirming much that they knew and some they'd guessed. He gave the location of Fargo's rendezvous with the German freighter. Then, with a malicious grin at Ben, said:

"Fargo's this bird's brother!"

The Ensign turned a startled look on Ben. Ben kept his eyes on Yettem. "Yes?"

"Goddam right! You better be lockin' him up, too—he's in it with the rest of us!"

Still watching Yettem, Ben got his wallet from a pocket and handed it to the Commander. "You'll find my papers in there." He said tight-lipped to Yettem: "You better have proof of that, mister—"

"Proof?" Yettem laughed. "You know that my name's Reb Fargo, don't you? Your ol' man and my ol' woman got gay one night an'—"

The Ensign, watching Taylor, nodded to his men. Still spluttering, they led Yettem aft, ignoring his threats and curses. The Ensign said: "Nasty fellow," and went back to the bridge.

Incredible as it seemed, Ben knew that Yettem was right. Much that had been fogged in the past came suddenly clear. He saw now how that money his father had left in trust to send young Mace through college, like Taylor's last request, had been intended by his marshal father as a kind of atonement for the wrong he had done both the boy and old Fork Fargo.

And one other thing Ben understood. With a crystal clarity he saw that, richly as the man deserved it, he could not kill Mace Fargo now.

Barely moving, the cutter continued on its course.

The Ensign said when Ben rejoined him: "This lad"—indicating the quartermaster at the helm—

"is the best navigator on the whole west coast. He can find anything in the Pacific larger than a flea; he'll find that tub for us without hardly working up a sweat."

The tide had changed; it was strong off shore. The helmsman reported their position as being within one half mile of the cruiser's suspected rendezvous; and almost instantly the lookout's voice called guardedly: "Light ahead, sir!"

The Ensign, leaning forward, held a muttered consultation. The quartermaster calculated their position, estimated the drift and flow of tide with a seamanlike precision. The Ensign nodded, tersely gave his orders. The great blue engines ceased their pulsing. The binnacle was dimmed and like a phantom ship they drifted silently, slow but surely, down upon the cruiser's anchorage.

Yettem, brought from the brig, gave assurance of the craft's identity. The Ensign said, "We'll board her!" and called for volunteers.

Closer and closer the unsuspecting ship they crept on the offshore tide. Not until the cutter actually loomed above the cruiser's bow was it spotted. The fenders bumped. From the rail Ben sprang in a mighty leap even as the cruiser's lookout choked a startled curse. A right to the jaw sent the fellow sprawling. Ben hurled himself at the ladder, went down it like a hawk. An open rectangle loomed before him and he went through it, bare-lipped and with Bella's ringing scream in his ears. Fargo's first frantic shot scraped red across his cheek. Then only arm's length was between them and Ben was onto him, smashing hard knuckles against his mouth.

But Fargo was a bull for strength. He was desperate, was fighting for his life and knew it.

Ben staggered, half stunned by a blow from Fargo's pistol. Again that flashing barrel struck and all Ben's muscles fell apart. There was no will left in him. The room was a crazy, spinning, red-fogged blur and his legs were buckling under him when a shoulder struck the near bulkhead.

He caught at it, clutched it, somehow hung there, swaying, fighting to get the breath back into his lungs. Fargo's face was a blood-streaked blur. Straight before him it was, the willful lips drawn back in leering mockery, the eyes triumphant. The gleam of metal lifting in his fist keened Ben's gaze then and he got a foot up—shoved; saw Fargo lurching, doubled and gasping, back against the bed.

Thought of Bella drove Ben forward, cleared the fog from before his eyes. His swinging haymaker missed as Fargo spun to the left. Then Fargo was crouching. The gun in his fist was coming up as Ben hurled himself against him.

They struck the floor in a writhing tangle. The whole place shook. Desperation lent frantic speed to Fargo's need; he rolled on clear and clawed to a knee, one bracing hand spreading spatulate, steadying fingers against ship's planking while his other brought the pistol to deadly focus.

"Hold it!"

Fargo's eyes came up and widened. There was that moment of hesitation, then all the rage drained out of them, leaving them pale and beaten.

Behind Ben's shoulder a squad of Guardsmen stood with leveled rifles. The Ensign's face was whitely set.

Fargo let his pistol drop.

The paper king was beaten, his paper kingdom fallen.

They led him off. Ben turned then to find Bella watching him, her eyes still wide, still incredulous. Even yet, it seemed, she could not believe he was alive. He came before her, watching her face swing up, his bloodshot eyes showing a little wistful as her hand came up and softly touched his cheek.

Then she was in his arms, was sobbing with her head against his chest. He put his good arm around her, knowing why she cried; knowing that when her tears had ended she would have put the past with all its heartaches and misery back of her, forever.

She looked up at him, smiling through her tears. Her lips came up and his lips met them . . . and for these two, in all the world, there was nothing else that mattered.

About the Author

Nelson C. Nye was born in Chicago, Illinois, educated in schools in Ohio and Massachusetts, and attended the Cincinnati Art Academy. His early journalism experience was writing publicity releases and book reviews for the *Cincinnati Times-Star* and the *Buffalo Evening News*. In 1935, he began working as a ranch hand in Texas and California and became an expert on breeding quarter horses on his own ranch outside Tucson, Arizona. Much of this love for horses can be found in exceptional novels like *Wild Horse Shorty* and *Blood of Kings*. He published his first Western short story in *Thrilling Western* and his first Western novel in 1936. He continued from then on to write prolifically, both under his own name and the bylines Drake C. Denver and Clem Colt.

During World War II, he served with the U. S. Army Field Artillery. From 1949 to 1952, he worked as horse editor for *Texas Livestock Journal*. He was one of the founding members of the Western Writers of America in 1953 and served twice as its president. His first Golden Spur Award from the Western Writers of America came to him for best Western reviewer and critic in 1954. From 1958 to 1962, he was the frontier fiction reviewer for the *New York Times Book Review*. His second Golden Spur came for his novel, *Long Run*. His virtues as an author of Western fiction include a tremendous sense of authenticity, an ability to keep the pace of a story from lagging, and a rich inventiveness for plot twists and situations. Some of his finest novels have had off-trail protagonists such as *The Barber of Tubac*, while both *Not Grass Alone* and *Strawberry Roan* are notable for their outstanding female characters. His books have sold over 50,000,000 copies worldwide and have been translated into multiple languages. *The Los Angeles Times* once praised him for his "marvelous lingo, salty humor, and real characters." Above all, a Western story by Nelson C. Nye possesses a vital energy that is both propulsive and persuasive.

Center Point Large Print
600 Brooks Road / PO Box 1
Thorndike, ME 04986-0001 USA

(207) 568-3717

**US & Canada:
1 800 929-9108**
www.centerpointlargeprint.com